'I'm asking **because it's** **like your con** **to come or no**

'Yes,' said Kate, and he kissed her square on her surprised mouth.

'I'll pick you up just before seven and feed you after the show.' Ben laid a finger on her lower lip, smiled at her, then leaned across to undo her seatbelt.

Kate shrank back into her seat, away from the warmth and scent of his body, afraid he'd realise how his nearness affected her.

'Stop it,' he said sternly, sitting upright. 'You're in no danger from me, I promise.'

That's the trouble, she thought ruefully. I wish I were.

Dear Reader,

Pennington, my favourite location, is my own creation. Having lived near two attractive country towns in the past, I combine the best features of both, not least the classical buildings and pump rooms dating from the Regency era, when spas were all the rage. My serene, fictional town has wide streets, teashops, public gardens ablaze with flowers, irresistible shops with elegant clothes and jewellery, others with bargains in antique furniture and porcelain. A centre for thriving businesses, yet set in rich agricultural land, Pennington is the dream combination of delightful people, prosperity and picturesque charm.

Yours sincerely,

Catherine George

Other *Pennington* stories by Catherine George:

AFTER THE BALL
SUMMER OF THE STORM
REFORM OF THE RAKE
EARTHBOUND ANGEL

There'll be another visit to *Pennington* soon. Watch out for the special flash on our covers!

NO MORE SECRETS

BY
CATHERINE GEORGE

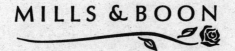

MILLS & BOON

All the characters in this book have no existence outside the imagination of the author, and have no relation whatsoever to anyone bearing the same name or names. They are not even distantly inspired by any individual known or unknown to the author, and all the incidents are pure invention.

*MILLS & BOON and the Rose Device
are trademarks of the publisher.
Harlequin Mills & Boon Limited,
Eton House, 18-24 Paradise Road, Richmond, Surrey TW9 1SR*

© Catherine George 1996

ISBN 0 263 79815 1

Set in Times Roman 10 on 12 pt.
02-9611-53130 C1

Made and printed in Great Britain

CHAPTER ONE

A SUDDEN squall of wind sent the yellow wool hat spinning across the road like a discus, and its small, hurrying owner dived after it in hot pursuit through a hail of sleet, blind to the oncoming car until it was almost on top of her with an ear-splitting squeal of brakes. Kate leapt away in fright, stumbled and fell on her hands and knees with a screech as the car swerved to avoid her and slewed sideways to a halt across the quiet backstreet.

The driver shot out and came running to pull her to her feet, his face haggard with shock. 'Are you hurt? You gave me one hell of a fright! I came round the corner and there you were, right in the middle of the road. Did I hit you?'

Kate shook her head, half-blinded by wind and sleet and the strands of dark hair whipping across her face, speechless not only from shock but also from confrontation with the most attractive man she'd ever laid eyes on in her life. 'Sorry—my fault entirely,' she gasped. 'Wind blew my hat off. I ran into the road after it. The car didn't even touch me. Must dash.'

He retrieved the hat and handed it back to her. 'Look, let me drive you—' he began, but Kate backed away, shaking her head vigorously.

'No, thanks, I'm fine! Really. My apologies again. Goodbye.'

She gave him a brief, embarrassed smile and raced off round the corner into the Parade before the man could do anything to prevent her.

When Kate arrived, panting, at the bookshop she felt more than a little shaky. What a start! Especially on an important day like this. But she just had to pull herself together, put the incident from her mind. She rummaged for her keys with unsteady hands, making herself concentrate on the display in the largest window. She took a few deep breaths and gave a nod of approval. The display was definitely eye-catching, bound to bring the punters in. The publicity stills of Quinn Fletcher, best-selling crime novelist and local celebrity, were good. Beauty and crime were a great combination for selling books. And books might be Kate Harker's passion, but selling them was her job.

Luckily for her wind and limb she had set out a good hour earlier than usual, determined to make sure everything was perfect for the book-signing later on. Rush-hour traffic could have turned an embarrassing little incident into a nasty accident, but, thankfully, the quiet backstreet had been deserted. And now, she thought irritably, she'd have to utilise some of the time to make herself look more presentable. She was a mess. She shivered suddenly. If the car had been speeding round the corner, or if the driver's reactions had been slower, she could have been looking far more of a mess than she did now.

When all the lights in the store were on Kate started up the electronic point-of-sale system at the till, took the money and till drawers from the safe in the office and installed them at the sales desks. By the time the rest of the staff arrived both the new floor manager and the shop itself were in readiness for the day. Kate had re-placed muddied jeans with a skirt, and restored face and hair to the severe, businesslike look she kept to during working hours.

Teased about her early start, Kate smiled cheerfully, glad of the camaraderie. She'd arrived in Pennington to take over the post of floor manager only a few weeks before, and to her relief her new colleagues were a pleasant crew, with no hint of hostility from one or two who might have expected promotion to her job.

Her career with Hardacres had begun as a junior bookseller at their Kensington branch a year after gaining her English degree. After leaving university she'd worked at whatever job she could until winning the post with the successful chain of specialist bookstores. Kate's pro-motion to senior bookseller had been gratifyingly rapid, but in the Kensington flagship branch further pro-motion to floor manager would have been slower. So when the opening in the Pennington branch came up Kate had applied, eager to make a move she welcomed in more ways than one.

At first, in a town where the architecture was beautiful but everyone was a stranger, Kate had missed her life in London badly, and regretted her decision. Then she'd found a permanent place to live, made some successful decisions about new titles, contacted Quinn Fletcher's publishers about the book-signing opportunity, and begun to enjoy her new life. Pennington was a less ex-pensive place to live for a start, which made her salary go further. And the slower pace rather suited her. The other girls at Hardacres were friendly, the job was in-teresting and varied, and no one made demands on either

her time or her emotions. It was surprisingly restful. The move, she'd decided eventually, had been a good idea.

Kate tidied the fiction shelves, checked to see if any titles needed re-ordering, made sure someone was at the till in her department during the break period, then went for coffee herself once Gail, who was so pretty that male college students crowded the store when she was on duty, was back at the till.

'I brought some scones my mother made,' said Gail, flicking back a lock of glossy blonde hair. 'I saved one for you, Kate.'

Kate, perpetually struggling with one diet or another, thanked her ruefully. In the staffroom she poured herself some coffee from the machine, scowling at the buttered scone.

'Eat,' said Clare, the language specialist. 'You seem a bit edgy.'

Kate described her near-miss with a Range Rover that morning, pulling a face as she admitted it was all her own fault in her hurry to get to work. 'I wanted an hour to myself to make sure everything was perfect. It's the book signing. I've never actually organised one before.' Succumbing to temptation, Kate bit into the scone and sighed with pleasure. 'I just wish Gail's mother wasn't such a cracking cook!'

'A fright like that probably burned up enough calories to account for one scone! Heavens, Kate, you were lucky.' Clare patted her arm. 'And don't worry about Quinn Fletcher. She sells like hot cakes—amazingly gory stuff, too.'

'I know. I've read them all. This last one's the best yet. I gather she's married?'

Clare nodded. 'I'm almost as new in town as you, so I don't know him, but he's gorgeous, according to Gail. Some people get all the luck.'

'You've got a gorgeous husband yourself!' retorted Kate.

'But I don't write best-sellers.'

'True.' Kate jumped up. 'I'd better tidy myself up— again—and make sure everything's ready. Make sure there's a fresh pot of coffee on the go for Ms Fletcher, there's a dear.'

'Don't worry. Tray all ready with best cups and luxury biscuits. But no scones. Young Harry scoffed the last one and had to be forcibly prevented from thieving yours.'

'I wish he had!' Kate smoothed her long grey flannel skirt over hips too curvy for her taste, brushed a stray strand of hair into her severe pleat of hair and replaced the horn-rimmed glasses she wore during working hours. She renewed her lipstick, tucked her striped grey and white shirt in more securely, and buttoned the grey waistcoat bought to hide the opulence of her upper half. 'There. How do I look?'

'Frighteningly efficient,' Clare assured her, chuckling. She stood up, stretching, long-legged and slim in jeans and navy jersey. And tall.

It was Kate's misfortune to have joined a team where every other member, male and female, were well over average height. Her own five feet and a bit was no match for Clare and Gail, and certainly not Harry, who was a gangling six-footer and still growing. Even Mrs Harrison, the manager, was a head taller.

'I didn't realise you had such great legs,' commented Clare, attending to the coffee-pot. 'Never seen them before.'

They all habitually wore trousers or jeans, with shirts and jerseys of various descriptions, because the work entailed a lot of kneeling and hefting around of boxes by all the staff. But today Kate felt the occasion called for a skirt. Which, though long and narrow, with a rather dashing split to the knee, felt dowdy alongside the leggy Clare and tall, slender Gail.

'I'll change back into my usual gear once our celebrity's departed,' she said, and went out into the store, glad to see several customers browsing in all sections of her department. By the time she'd found various titles for some of them, directed Harry to help Gail when necessary, and checked that the table and chairs for the signing were in a prominent place, ready for the author, it was almost eleven.

Clocks in the town were chiming the hour when a car drew up outside. Kate went to the door, her smile ready in welcome, then caught her breath in dismay as a tall man with an unmistakable shock of blond hair leapt out to help his companion to her feet. The woman's brown curls and laughing, flushed face were equally recognisable from the photographs in the display; but with one noticeable difference.

'Oh, crikey,' breathed Clare. 'She's pregnant. *Very* pregnant.'

Kate braced herself and went forward, hand outstretched. 'Ms Fletcher? I'm Kate Harker. Welcome to Hardacres.'

'Thank you. You're new.' Quinn Fletcher shook Kate's hand, smiling warmly. 'Charlie's left?'

Kate nodded. 'Mr Walters went to manage the Oxford branch.'

'You're much prettier than Charlie Walters!' The man grinned down at her, then narrowed his eyes, frowning, and Kate turned away hurriedly.

Behind her calm, efficient exterior she felt depressed. So her rescuer was married. And even more handsome than she'd remembered from the fleeting episode in the pouring rain. But he was years younger than his wife—which, of course, was absolutely nothing to do with Kate Harker. 'Please come inside,' she urged, smiling brightly. 'There's a very cold wind today.'

'Better than the sleet earlier,' he returned with a grin, and turned to shepherd his companion inside with care. 'You all right, love?'

'Fine.' Quinn Fletcher smiled at him reassuringly. 'You can pop off now, Ben, if you like.'

He shook his head as he helped her to settle in the chair behind the small table used for signings. 'No way. I'm here to keep an eye on you. Don't worry, if I get bored there's plenty to read!'

Quinn Fletcher smiled up at him lovingly. 'Fusspot!' She turned to Kate. 'Take no notice. The baby's not due for weeks yet.'

Kate, up to then convinced that the baby's arrival was imminent, relaxed a little. 'Before you start would you like some coffee?'

The attractive author shook her head regretfully. 'Later, if that's all right. If I have one now I'll be making more trips to the bathroom than signing books—always supposing someone wants to buy—' She broke off with a smile as she realised a line was already forming. 'Oh, how lovely. Look at all these people! Let's get started.'

Quinn Fletcher was kept busy with her fountain-pen as she smiled and chatted to each customer eager for her signature, most of them fans eagerly awaiting the latest best-selling thriller from a novelist who was popular worldwide, as well as in her home town of Pennington.

'Mr Fletcher, would you like some coffee?' asked Kate.

'Thanks, I would.' He turned away from a display of paperback novels, smiling down at her. 'I skipped breakfast.' He paused, one surprisingly dark eyebrow raised. 'How do you feel? None the worse for your adventure this morning, I hope?'

'No, not in the least,' said Kate, resigned. 'I thought perhaps you hadn't recognised me.'

'It took a while,' he agreed, his smile deepening. 'The disguise is good.'

'No disguise.' Her hackles rose at the hint of intimacy in the dark, dancing eyes. 'This is how I normally look.'

'Why?' he countered. 'I preferred you the other way.'

Kate, longing to give a stinging set-down to Quinn Fletcher's husband, was forced to give him a polite little smile instead before going off to fetch the coffee. She felt oddly let down, she realised, irritated with herself. And not just because Ben Fletcher was married, either. She strongly disapproved of a man ready to indulge in a spot of flirtation right under the nose of his heavily pregnant wife.

'Crumbs,' said Clare, following her in. 'Can I give Mr Fletcher the coffee, boss? He's *seriously* gorgeous.'

'And you're married,' retorted Kate.

'But not blind.' Clare smacked her lips as she hefted a small tray. 'Besides, I'm more his size than you are.'

Kate grinned, yanked her waistcoat straight, and returned to the fray, where a gratifyingly long line was still snaking through the front of the store. Leaving Clare to supply the spectacular Mr Fletcher's needs, she went to the till to give Harry and Gail a hand as they took the money for *The Letting of Blood*. She felt a glow of satisfaction as she packed books into smart black bags with a plain gilt H. Most of the customers had bought other books as well as the new thriller. She glanced over at the author. Half-hidden behind the table, in a loose white coat, Quinn Fletcher's condition wasn't evident to the waiting fans. Somehow one didn't expect a writer of frankly gory thrillers to be pregnant. Or to have such a young Adonis of a husband, either. One who apparently had nothing to do other than to escort his wife to a book-signing, chat up every female in sight—and laugh all the way to the bank when he deposited her royalty cheques, no doubt. Kate put on hasty mental brakes. None of her business.

She beckoned to Clare. 'Would you take over from Gail for ten minutes, please? Gail, see if Ms Fletcher needs a drink yet, then take a break.'

Gail relinquished her place to Clare eagerly, and went over to Quinn Fletcher, who shook her head, smiling, apparently quite unconcerned when her husband turned the full battery of his charm on the pretty blonde bookseller.

Kate turned away to deal with a customer, deeply sorry for Quinn Fletcher. The husband was a menace to anything young and female, obviously, pregnant wife or not.

After an hour Kate went over to the table.

'Time for a break? You look tired.'

'I think she's had enough,' put in Ben Fletcher, 'though she won't admit it while there's someone brandishing a book at her.'

'I'm fine,' said Quinn firmly, and smiled across the table at the elderly lady holding out a book. 'Hello; how nice of you to come.'

It was another half-hour before the last fan had gone happily away. Ben Fletcher helped the author to her feet with a solicitude which set Kate's teeth on edge. Hypocrite!

'Honestly, Cass,' said Ben Fletcher, frowning, 'you look done in. Come on, I'll take you home.'

Quinn Fletcher's smile was warmly reassuring, despite the smudges of fatigue beneath her eyes. 'What I need first is a visit to the loo, then a sit down in a comfortable chair. *Then* you can drive me home.'

Kate led her to the staffroom, showed her the Ladies', checked the coffee was fresh and hot, then waited until Quinn Fletcher emerged, and pulled forward a solid leather chair. 'We all fight over this one, it's so comfortable. Coffee?'

'I shouldn't, but I will.' The novelist sat down, leaning back with a sigh.

'I hope all this wasn't too much for you,' said Kate, pouring out. 'I didn't know you were pregnant.'

'Don't worry, I'm fine. A book-signing session won't do me any harm.' She smiled. 'My small son wears me out far more. Angus is three and gorgeous, but lord is he energetic! How I ever got this book finished I'll never know. Luckily I've got a brilliant girl who comes in for a few hours a week to give me a hand with young Angus after nursery-school hours, otherwise I'd never have made my deadline.'

'Ms Fletcher—'

'Call me Cassie. Quinn's my pen name.'

Kate smiled warmly, very taken with the author's charm. 'I just wanted to say I'm one of your fans. I've read all your books, but I left my copy of this one at home. I read it over the weekend. Some time, when you're in town, would you mind calling in to sign it for me?'

'Of course; I'd be glad to.' Cassie Fletcher finished her coffee and got to her feet carefully. 'Right, then, Kate Harker, I must be off. Could you round up Ben for me?'

Ben Fletcher was discovered in a far corner of the store, handing up books for a very excited, pink-faced Gail to stack on a high shelf.

'Incorrigible,' said Cassie, looking resigned rather than annoyed.

Kate, annoyed for her, moved over to the industrious pair, who were so absorbed with each other that neither noticed her arrival. 'Ms Fletcher is ready to leave now,' she said crisply. 'Gail, if you've finished there the children's corner could do with some tidying.'

'Yes, Kate,' said Gail, and went off precipitately, blushing to the roots of her hair.

Ben Fletcher watched her go, frowning. 'I hope I didn't get her into trouble. I was just giving a helping hand.'

'Not at all. Very kind of you,' said Kate politely, and walked ahead of him to the signing table, where the author was taking leave of the manager and the other members of staff.

'Ah, there you are, Ben,' said Cassie Fletcher. 'Sorry to keep you hanging round so long.'

'My pleasure, love.' He grinned. 'I found ways to pass the time.'

There was a chorus of farewells as the writer promised to come back the following year when her next novel came out. Ben Fletcher bestowed his dazzling smile on everyone except Kate, who won an oddly wry, questioning glance before he escorted Cassie to the car parked outside.

Mrs Harrison congratulated Kate on a very successful signing session, and the others returned to their various tasks—except for a rather wary Gail.

'Kate, I'm down for early lunch today, but could I go late instead, please?'

'I'll swap,' offered Harry promptly. 'I'm starving.'

'Yes, fine,' said Kate rather coolly. 'Stay at the till until one, then, Gail. Harry, put the table and chairs away first, then off you go.'

The staffroom was a comfortable, untidy place where all of them were glad to rest their tired feet, eat sandwiches and drink coffee, chat, read the paper, or just relax for the hour's break. Harry usually went out to join cronies for a pizza, but the female section of the staff tended to congregate together, glad to sit down.

Today Kate was not glad to sit down. For some reason she felt restless. Gail went out shopping, Mrs Harrison and Clare were grappling with *The Times* crossword, and after swallowing a sandwich and half a cup of coffee Kate excused herself to dash out and buy some shampoo. Somehow she couldn't bring herself to say she just needed to be out in the open air, though the sleet showers had given way to chilly sunshine by this time. She walked briskly, guilty enough about her excuse to walk to the other end of town and buy shampoo she didn't need. On her way back past public gardens bright with early daffodils, Kate eyed the tempting cakes in the corner coffee-shop with longing, wishing she had Clare's metabolism. Suddenly her eyes widened. At one of the tables inside the coffee-shop, clearly visible through the shelves of Danish pastries and cream buns, sat Gail, her eyes like stars as she gazed at the man with her. His back was turned to Kate, but it was all too easy to see that Gail's companion was Ben Fletcher.

The louse! thought Kate fiercely. Cassie Fletcher was at home, pregnant, coping with a boisterous toddler into the bargain, and here was Ben Fletcher chatting up young Gail, who, seemingly, was so taken with him she was prepared to overlook his married status.

Kate turned away sharply. It was none of her business. Not even Gail. Unless the girl's work suffered because of it her private life was her own affair, however she chose to conduct it. Kate cut across the gardens, taking the longest route possible back to the shop to calm down. It was Cassie she felt for. A warm, lovely lady like Cassie Fletcher deserved something better than a blond Romeo who reacted to every woman in sight. Well not *every* woman, amended Kate with painful honesty. She was the only one he hadn't smiled at on leaving, so it was obvious she didn't merit the Ben Fletcher gold seal of approval.

The afternoon was busy, as usual. Kate spent a large part of it with a publishing rep, discussing new titles for the summer list, then did some chasing up on book deliveries to make sure they arrived for various special displays she was organising. In between she helped customers find titles they were looking for, tidied up the children's corner after the usual post-school surge of mothers and offspring and kept a general eagle eye on everything going on in her department. By the time her shift ended just before seven Kate had managed to push thoughts of the Fletchers to the back of her mind, even able to bid Gail a fairly affable goodnight instead of wringing her neck, as she'd wanted to earlier.

It was almost dark and raining again when she set out to walk to the older part of Pennington. Kate pulled the stitched brim of the now dry wool hat low over her eyes, buttoned her raincoat to the neck and set off at a brisk pace.

Shortly after her arrival in Pennington she'd answered an advertisement which required 'a young professional lady for a small flat in a house off Waverley Square'. Kate had gone to inspect it without much hope, but had been charmed by the house, which was small, flat-roofed, and one of a pair in a quiet cul-de-sac tucked away behind a row of imposing Georgian mansions. Waverley Lodge had a small front garden with shrubs and a lilac tree, and the flat, Kate had learned, was the entire upper floor of the house. Mrs Beaumont, the owner, was a sprightly lady in her late seventies, with curly white hair and shrewd dark eyes. She leaned heavily on a stick and could no longer manage stairs, she'd explained.

'My son and his wife want me to move into a modern flat, but I like it here. In common with that lilac tree I'm too old to transplant. But I would like some company in the house so I decided to let the upper floor.' Mrs Beaumont waved Kate upstairs. 'Look around all you want, my dear. Mrs Gill, my daily, assures me it's all spick and span up there. Come down when you're ready and I'll make some tea.'

Kate thanked her and went off to inspect the upper floor of Waverley Lodge. A bright, airy sitting room, with comfortable, chintz-covered furniture, lots of lamps, bookshelves and small tables, looked out over a quiet square with a lawn and trees softening the view of tall, aristocratic houses on the far side, a view shared by the pleasant double bedroom. A pretty bathroom, plus a small kitchen converted from what must once have been a boxroom, looked out on the small garden of the Lodge.

As she hurried in the direction of Waverley Lodge now it seemed hard to realise it had been her home for less than a month. Kate and Mrs Beaumont had taken to each other on sight. Which, as the old lady had explained, was why Kate was served tea that first day. None of the other applicants had qualified for it.

'I agree with George—my son—that it's a shame to leave the rooms empty,' Mrs Beaumont had said, 'but I couldn't share my home with someone I didn't—well, *fancy*. And some young people dress very oddly these days.'

Kate, it seemed, had passed the test on sight. And she was glad of it. The rent for the rooms in Waverley Lodge was steeper than she'd hoped, but with care, and some cutting down in other directions, she could manage it. The only drawback was the lack of a separate entrance.

'I do like to go out at night sometimes,' Kate had warned. 'I'm doing a course in business studies two nights a week, and I like the cinema and the theatre. Won't it disturb you when I come in?'

Mrs Beaumont had assured her that it would not. She would like having someone young about the house. If Kate had any doubts they would give it a month's trial and see how things went. So far things had gone so well that Kate hated the idea of finding another place. At first she'd been sure she'd miss the untidy flat she'd

shared with three other girls in Putney. But to her surprise this wasn't the case at all. She found she enjoyed
her new-found privacy and orderliness more than the
previous casual companionship. She could choose what
programmes she liked on the radio and television, and
read in peace whenever she wanted, which was a vital
part of her job, since the fiction section of the store was
her own particular responsibility. There was no race for
the bathroom, or unwashed dishes in the kitchen sink,
and, best of all, no embarrassing little encounters with
strange young men on the landing first thing in the
morning.

Kate was so lost in thoughts of her former existence,
head bowed against the wind, that she cannoned straight
into the man emerging from the indoor car park she
passed on the way home every night.

'Sorry!' she gasped, pushing her hat out of her eyes,
then stiffened, pulling away from the hands holding her
by the elbows.

'Miss Harker again, no less,' drawled Ben Fletcher,
releasing her. 'You don't suffer from a death-wish, by
any chance? Or are you blind without those enormous
glasses?'

'Neither—I'm just in a hurry to get home. I'm afraid
I didn't notice you,' she said coldly.

His grin surprised her. It was very different from the
one he turned on like a light to charm. 'Which puts me
in my place. I'm not *very* vain, but people usually notice
me.'

Wasn't that the truth, thought Kate, remembering the
scene in the coffee-shop, and tried to pass him, but to
her annoyance he caught her wrist.

'Wait. Have we met before today?' he asked.

'No.'

'Then why do I get the feeling you disapprove of me? Do you bear a grudge because I almost ran you over? I thought perhaps you knew me from somewhere, and felt annoyed because I'd forgotten.'

Kate looked pointedly at the fingers on her wrist and Ben Fletcher dropped his hand. 'You're mistaken on both counts, Mr Fletcher. I don't know you.' And don't want to, implied her tone so clearly that his eyes narrowed for a moment, then danced in a way which made her long to hit out at him.

'I hear you loud and clear, Miss Harker. Pity. Cassie liked you very much, incidentally. And just in case you were wondering,' he added, 'she suffered no ill effects from the signing.'

'Good; I'm very glad. Goodnight, Mr Fletcher.'

Ben Fletcher gazed down at her thoughtfully, making it impossible to dash off as Kate wanted.

'By the way,' he said casually, 'how long have you lived in Pennington?'

Kate frowned. 'Just under a month.'

'Ah. New kid on the block.' He raised his hand in salute. 'Well, can't hang about enjoying myself like this—got someone to meet. Goodnight.'

Kate nodded coldly and walked off at a furious rate, fairly sure he was watching her go. At last she gave in to temptation and risked a peek over her shoulder. And then wished she hadn't. Far from watching her out of sight, Ben Fletcher was striding towards the girl waiting outside Hardacres. A girl with hair as bright as his own, who rushed to meet him. Gail again.

Kate turned on her heel, almost running in an effort to put as much space between herself and the happy pair

who were obviously about to spend the evening together.
Did Cassie Fletcher *know* what the man was doing while
she was putting their son to bed, or cooking dinner, or
whatever she was likely to be doing at this time of night?

Kate arrived precipitately at the door of Waverley
Lodge, glad to reach her flat without encountering Mrs
Beaumont. As she peeled off her wet raincoat and hung
it up in the bathroom to dry she felt very out of sorts.
The Fletchers were none of her business. Before this
morning she'd never met either of them. But, as a
firsthand witness to Ben Fletcher's infidelity, Kate felt
horribly responsible in some way. Which was ridiculous.
Besides, she was unlikely to meet Cassie Fletcher again.
And even if she did Kate knew she'd never tell Cassie
her husband was cheating on her. No way was she ever
getting involved in anyone else's affairs again.

CHAPTER TWO

KATE forced herself to say nothing to Gail on the subject of married men. Gail might well misconstrue her motives, put it down to jealousy, and the girl knew Ben Fletcher was married anyway, so it was useless to point out something so obvious. And Gail was so patently moonstruck about him that she'd never believe Kate preferred dark, lean, witty types, whose attraction was a lot more cerebral than the up-front charms of Cassie Fletcher's husband, damn the man.

How could a clever, mature lady like Cassie be attracted to someone like Ben Fletcher? Kate was haunted by the thought for a day or two, until two evening classes added to a very busy working week tired her out so much that there was no room in her thoughts for anything other than the exam she must pass fairly soon.

'You work hard,' observed Mrs Beaumont as they drank coffee together the following Sunday morning.

'But I love it. One day I'm going to manage one of the big London bookshops,' Kate confided.

'Good for you. Life in Pennington must be a bit slow after London.'

'No. Oddly enough it isn't. Different, of course, but I find I like life in a shire town—the change of pace is rather welcome.'

'Good. Oh, by the way, dear,' said Mrs Beaumont, 'I'm going away to my sister's in Bath for a few days tomorrow. Mrs Gill will be in to clean as usual. She keeps a key.'

Mondays were demanding for Kate. After her stint at the shop she hastily ate a sandwich and went straight on to her evening class. By the time she arrived home that night it was oddly dismaying to find the house in darkness. She unlocked the door and ran upstairs to her flat, turning on lamps everywhere, careless for once of the electricity bill. She put cottage cheese, tomatoes and a thin slice of ham on a plate, added a couple of crisp-breads and an apple, and went to curl up on the sofa in the sitting room to eat her frugal meal in front of the television news.

Afterwards, still hungry but determined to ignore it, Kate took the pins out of her hair, ran a bath and sank into it with a sigh of relief as she settled down to read. This was another advantage of having a flat to herself. In Putney someone had always banged on the door if she took longer than a few minutes over a bath.

Eventually, yawning, she washed her hair, wrapped herself in the new yellow towelling robe her mother had given her for Christmas, and went back to the sitting room to dry her hair while she finished the newest best-seller on display at Hardacres.

By eleven Kate's long dark hair was dry enough to let her go to bed. She fell asleep almost the moment her head touched the pillow, then woke later with a start, her heart beating rapidly. She lay still, hardly daring to breathe. Someone was moving about downstairs. Her instinct was to pull the covers over her ears and hope the burglar would go away. But he was stealing Mrs Beaumont's treasures. Worse still, he might come up-stairs for more.

She slid stealthily out of bed, took a heavy wooden book-end from a shelf, then tiptoed out onto the landing. The burglar was making no attempt to be quiet, she noted, shivering, and, taking a deep breath, she crept down, missile at the ready. As she reached the bend in the stairs a man emerged from Mrs Beaumont's sitting room, and, giving herself no time to think, Kate let fly with the book-end and caught him fair and square on the temple. The man dropped like a stone to the Persian carpet, and lay still.

Kate gave a squawk of horror and ran to him, falling on her knees beside the motionless figure. She seized his wrist, searching wildly for his pulse. Relief flooded her as it throbbed reassuringly against her fingers. She stared down at him in dismay, wondering what on earth to do. He was young, dark and sharp-featured, and remarkably well dressed for a burglar. And he wasn't dead. Something he confirmed by opening dazed dark eyes to stare into her tense face.

'Don't move,' she ordered in a shaking voice. 'Stay where you are. I've called the police.'

'What the hell did you hit me with?' he demanded irritably, struggling up despite her efforts to prevent him. 'Have I been out long?'

'Ten minutes,' lied Kate. 'Stay where you are!'

To her astonishment he began to laugh.

'You won't find it so funny when the police come!' she snapped furiously. 'You should be ashamed of yourself, trying to rob an elderly lady—'

'I wasn't robbing her—I'm trying to find her glasses,' he said unsteadily, taking the wind out of Kate's sails. 'My name's Daniel Beaumont. Grandson of your landlady,' he added.

'How do I know?' she demanded fiercely, then picked up the book-end menacingly as he put a hand in his breast pocket.

'Don't hit me again—please,' he pleaded, putting up his hands in mock surrender. 'I'm unarmed, I swear. If you'll let me take out my wallet I can prove my identity.'

'All right,' she conceded. 'But no tricks.'

'Would I dare?' He winced, fingering his temple with one hand as he withdrew his wallet and tossed it over to her.

Kate flipped it open, and saw an identity card for the firm of Beaumont Electronics, with a photograph of the intruder, and the name Daniel Beaumont underneath it. Since there were also several credit cards and a business card for confirmation, she put the wallet down on the hall table and placed the book-end beside it, furiously embarrassed.

'You can get up now,' she said tartly.

Daniel Beaumont scrambled to his feet, a hand to his head. 'I really am very sorry for giving you a fright. I clean forgot Grandma had let the upper floor. The house was in darkness so I just used Dad's key and came to search for her glasses. I'm to post them on to Bath in the morning.'

'Did you have to come here at this time of night?' demanded Kate, unappeased.

'I had dinner with a friend and saw her home first.' He swayed a little. 'Look, would you mind if I sat down for a bit?'

Kate, secretly filled with remorse, took his arm and helped him into Mrs Beaumont's sitting room. 'All right. Sit down on the sofa there for a minute.'

'Brandy?' he said hopefully.

'Certainly not. You might be concussed.' She eyed him uncertainly. 'In fact, perhaps you ought to see a doctor, or go to the local casualty department.'

'No,' he said firmly. 'A hot cup of tea would be nice. Then I'll drive home and leave you in peace.'

Something in his bright, dark eyes reminded Kate that her only garment was a nightgown—dark green, winterweight and modestly voluminous, but still a nightgown.

'Sit still,' she ordered, and ran upstairs, put a kettle on to boil, and wrapped herself in her yellow robe. More shaken by the episode than she wanted to admit, she thrust her feet into espadrilles then set a tray with cups and for once made tea properly in a pot. She added sugar, milk, then took the tray downstairs to Mrs Beaumont's sitting room and put it down on a small table. Daniel Beaumont watched her, his eyes bright in his pale face, one of them showing signs of a bruise, courtesy of the book-end.

'I'm afraid you'll have a black eye,' said Kate without sympathy. 'Milk? Sugar?'

'Both, please.' He grinned ruefully. 'No one will believe I was mugged by a girl.'

She handed him a cup and saucer, then poured tea for herself and perched on the edge of an armchair opposite him. 'Mr Beaumont—'

'My name's Dan,' he interrupted. 'Won't you tell me yours?'

'Kate Harker. I'm sorry I hit you, but under the circumstances—'

'You had every right,' he assured her. 'You're a plucky girl, Kate Harker. But next time just ring the police. Don't come investigating yourself.'

'I lied about the police,' she confessed. 'I didn't have time to call them.'

'I know. I looked at my watch. I was only out for a second or two.' He drained his cup, looking rather better. 'Is there more, please?'

Kate refilled his cup, then sat back. 'Your grandmother talks about you. But I took it for granted you were a schoolboy.'

The corners of his wide, expressive mouth went down. 'Grandma tends to forget I'm a responsible adult now—'

'I wonder why,' said Kate drily, and he grinned.

'*Touché.*' He looked up as the clock in the hall struck one. 'Hell, I'm sorry. You must be tired. I'll go.' He stood up, swayed, then smiled bravely. 'There. Steady as a rock.'

Kate shook her head. 'Sit down again. I'll ring for a taxi.'

Dan Beaumont sat down so promptly that Kate suspected he felt far less chipper than he was making out. Annoyed because she felt guilty, she went to the telephone in the hall and rang an all-night taxi firm.

'Ten minutes,' she announced, returning to her uninvited visitor, who used the time profitably by telling her that he worked in his father's electronics firm.

'Dad runs the shooting match but I sell the product. I'm the marketing man.'

Kate could well believe it. Even on such short acquaintance Dan Beaumont was plainly the type to sell snowballs to an Eskimo.

'So reciprocate,' he demanded. 'What do you do, Kate Harker?'

'Sell books at Hardacres,' she replied, looking up with relief at a ring on the doorbell. 'Right, here's your lift home.'

Dan Beaumont rose to his feet, swayed a little, and Kate rushed to take his arm. He leaned on her heavily as she supported him to the door, then took her breath away by planting a swift kiss on her mouth before sprinting down the path with no trace of unsteadiness. She glared from the doorway as he saluted smartly, grinning all over his thin, confident face as he jumped in the cab.

Kate slammed the door and collected the tray, took it upstairs, washed up and climbed into bed with a groan. Only six hours to go before she had to get up again. And to make it worse the incident had left her wide awake and nervous. So much so that in the end she went downstairs again to make sure the front door was safely locked and bolted. At which point it occurred to her that Dan Beaumont's key had to be to the back door, which had no bolts, as she knew from Mrs Beaumont, so that her daily, Mrs Gill, could gain entry at any time. Kate turned the key in the back door, pushed a chair under the handle, and for the third time that night climbed wearily into bed.

Inevitably Kate slept late next morning, and had to skip breakfast to get to work on time.

'Crumbs, Kate,' said Harry as she let him in. 'You look terrible.'

'Thanks,' said Kate drily, and turned to greet Gail, who looked anything but terrible. So blooming, in fact, that Kate found it hard to be civil.

A few minutes later Mrs Harrison, having called Kate up to her office to discuss the day's expected deliveries,

eyed her with concern. 'Not coming down with something, dear, are you?'

Kate shook her head. 'Bad night. Which is unusual.
I normally sleep like a log.'

'Take it easy today, then. Get Harry to do the heavy
stuff. And go and drink some coffee before you make
a start.'

Kate obeyed, glad of ten minutes' breather in the
staffroom before she coped with the day.

Clare came in, eyebrows raised at Kate's heavy-eyed
pallor. 'Hangover or flu?'

'Disturbed night.' Kate got up. 'I'm fine. I just needed
a shot of caffeine to get me going. I slept late this
morning—no breakfast.'

'Go easy on the dieting today—give your blood sugars
a chance,' advised Clare, with the confidence of someone
who could eat three cream buns at once and never gain
an ounce. She eyed Kate closely. 'What disturbed you?'

Kate had no time to explain. 'Long story. Tell you at
lunch.'

Halfway through the morning Kate was called to the
phone.

'Miss Harker? Kate? Quinn Fletcher here—Cassie. I'm
coming down your way later. Perhaps we could have a
sandwich lunch together—and I'll sign that book for
you.'

Kate went pink with pleasure. 'How very nice of you.
I'd love to. I'm on late lunch today—where would you
like to meet?'

'How about that coffee-shop on the corner near you—
the one with the gorgeous cakes?'

Kate returned to her fiction section, a smile on her
face as she helped a customer find the latest offering

from a favourite author. The woman bought two other books, thanked Kate for her help, then went to the cash desk to hand her money to Gail. Kate bit her lip, frowning. Gail!

She waited until the girl was free. 'You're taking early lunch today, Gail,' she stated rather than asked.

The girl smiled warmly. 'That's right, Kate. Unless you want me to swap?'

'No, no,' said Kate in relief. 'That's fine.' Having routed the spectre of running into Cassie's husband flirting with Gail over lunch, Kate relaxed a little, and went off to join Clare for mid-morning coffee.

'You look better,' the other girl commented as she poured.

'Quinn Fletcher's asked me to lunch,' said Kate. 'I've got my copy of her book ready for her autograph.' She eyed her jeans and navy jersey without pleasure. 'I wish I'd worn something else.'

Harry popped his red head round the door, grinning. 'Miss Kate Harker, you're wanted.'

Kate shot to her feet and followed Harry's lanky figure into the shop. 'Who?'

Harry waved to a tall, familiar figure immersed in a book of modern paintings.

'You asked for me?' Kate enquired, and Ben Fletcher turned, putting down the book with care.

'Good morning, Miss Harker. I had an appointment in town, so I volunteered to bring a message from Cassie. She's running a bit late. Could you make it one-fifteen?'

'Yes, of course. I'll wait for her in the coffee-shop.'

'Keep an eye on her, will you?' he asked soberly. 'She tends to overdo things. Nag her to go home and have a nap.'

'I can hardly do that, Mr Fletcher,' said Kate stiffly.

'It might come better from an outsider,' he said gloomily, apparently unaware that Gail was smiling with rather frenzied animation at a group of young male students at the cash desk. Suddenly he grinned all over his face as a man strolled into the shop with a large bouquet of flowers. 'Dan? What the hell are *you* doing here? Don't tell me you can read!'

Kate swallowed hard as Dan Beaumont stared at her blankly for a moment, then marched up to her and presented her with the bouquet, ignoring Ben Fletcher.

'With my apologies for last night,' he said, eyeing Kate's glasses and tightly coiled hair. 'You look— different.'

'So do you, old son,' said Ben Fletcher. 'I like the shiner. Someone's husband caught up with you at last?'

'Actually,' drawled Dan Beaumont, 'it was Miss Harker here who gave me the black eye. Totally undeserved, of course.'

Hideously aware that Harry, Clare and not least Gail were looking on with varying degrees of curiosity, Kate took the flowers, thanked Dan Beaumont punctiliously, said goodbye to both men and hurried off to the staffroom to put her unwanted tribute into water.

Fortunately the shop was too busy for some time for explanation, and it was only when Harry and Gail had gone out to lunch and she was helping Clare man the till that Kate was able to give her colleague a brief, edited version of the previous night's adventures. Clare was fascinated.

'You actually went downstairs and faced this man, thinking he was a burglar? You idiot, Kate. Anything could have happened.'

'But it didn't. Because Dan Beaumont wasn't a burglar.'

'True. Or things could have been a lot worse.' Clare grinned. 'His manly pride obviously wasn't hurt by being felled by a pint-sized little thing like you. Those flowers were expensive.'

'Unnecessary extravagance,' said Kate, and smiled at a customer. 'Biographies, sir? If you'll just follow me...'

Kate was sitting with a cup of black coffee when Cassie Fletcher arrived for lunch. Her big brown eyes lit up as she spotted her lunch guest.

'Sorry I'm a bit behind, Kate. My hospital appointment was a bit delayed.'

'I've only just got here myself. Busy morning.' Kate eyed her companion anxiously. 'Was everything all right?'

'Oh, yes. Emily and I are both in the pink.'

'Emily?'

'We know it's a girl. My husband's delighted, because he wants us to call it a day after this one.' Cassie pulled a face. 'He's right, of course. I'm nearly thirty-nine. Not that motherhood in the forties is the danger it used to be.' She picked up the menu. 'Let me treat you to something sinful.'

Over smoked salmon sandwiches and some wicked French pastries Kate found it very easy to talk to Cassie Fletcher, confiding that the staff at Hardacres were easy to work with and her landlady was a dear.

'But no boyfriend,' said Cassie bluntly.

'No. But in a way that's oddly restful.' Kate chuckled. 'In London I shared a flat with three other girls and we all had boyfriends and there was never a moment's peace. It was a madhouse.'

'But don't you miss that?'

'I did at first. But now I can read as much as I like—which I need to for my job and my business course. I've got to do my homework. I go to the cinema with Clare, one of my colleagues at the shop. Her husband is away a lot with his job and she's new here too and glad of an evening out. I like my life very much.'

Cassie looked thoughtful as she stirred her coffee. 'It all sounds a bit, well, *quiet* for a girl of your age. How old are you?'

'Twenty-seven.'

The brown eyes moved over Kate's severely coiled hair and the plain navy jersey. 'At least you're not wearing those owlish glasses today.'

Kate's lips twitched. 'You mean I'm a bit of a turn-off in the appearance department.'

Cassie laughed. 'How rude I am. Sorry. Only when I was young I used to scrape my hair back and try to look older too. I feel a certain kinship, I suppose.'

'My hair's long because it's cheaper to wear it that way than keep getting it cut, but I can't leave it hanging about in working hours. And the clothes are part of the job. I do a lot of kneeling and carrying books about, so my working clothes tend to be serviceable.'

Cassie nodded, looked at Kate contemplatively for a time, then reached for the book beside Kate's plate. 'Right. I'll sign this on one condition. Will you come to lunch on Sunday? Just a family roast; nothing formal. Please say yes.'

Kate said yes very promptly, then bit her lip at the thought of Cassie's husband.

'Now you're trying to think of some forgotten appointment so you can back out,' said Cassie percipiently.

'No. I'd love to come.' Kate rose. 'Sorry to dash off but I'm due back.'

'I'll just hang on here for a few minutes. My husband's collecting me.' Cassie grinned. 'I can't get behind a driving wheel very comfortably these days. About one on Sunday, then.'

'It's very kind of you,' said Kate with sincerity. 'Perhaps you might spare a minute to talk about your work. I'd love to hear how you construct those complex plots of yours. Today all I've done is talk about me.'

'I enjoyed it,' said Cassie firmly, and handed over a card. 'That's my business card, but my home address is on it. We'll look forward to seeing you—Angus adores having guests.'

Kate hurried back to the bookshop, deep in thought. She very much doubted that Ben Fletcher would be equally delighted to welcome her to lunch. But she would go because she really liked Cassie. Besides, Sundays tended to drag unless the weather was fine and she could go out walking. An invitation to lunch wasn't to be sneezed at.

It was almost seven that evening before Kate locked up the shop. As she checked everything was secure, and took a last look at the 'Book of the Month' display in the window, a figure appeared beside her, reflected in the glass, and Kate swung round in surprise. 'Mr Beaumont!'

'No. That's my father. I'm Dan.' He grinned at her, the black eye giving him a disreputable air that was at odds with his designer tailoring. As the wind blew along the street he drew the collar of his dark overcoat up and took her arm. 'I thought I'd walk you home, not only to collect my car, but also to cast myself at your mercy again.'

Since Kate was holding his spectacular flowers in the crook of her free arm it seemed rude to refuse. 'What's your problem this time?'

'The same one. After all the drama last night I forgot my grandmother's glasses. For pity's sake find them for me so I can send them off at first light, or she'll cut me out of her will!'

'I doubt it,' said Kate, shaking her head. 'But please hurry—I'm cold and hungry and I've got a lot of work to do.'

'Tonight?' he said, crestfallen. 'I was hoping you'd have dinner with me.'

'Sorry. Exams looming.'

'What are you studying?'

Kate explained. 'Which doesn't give me much time,' she concluded. 'When I took my English degree I was younger—and I wasn't working. This time it's more of a struggle. But I'll get there.'

Dan expressed his admiration in extravagant terms. When they arrived at the Lodge he unlocked the door for her, switched on the light and stood leaning in the doorway of the sitting room while Kate ran the spectacle case to earth.

'Eureka!' she said, finding it behind a pile of books on one of the tables. 'So your finances are safe after all.'

'I was joking about the will,' he said stiffly.

'Of course.' Kate smiled. 'And now I must put these gorgeous flowers in water. Thank you again. I hope the eye mends soon.'

'Let's talk about dinner again. Surely you don't work every night?'

'No. Two nights I go to classes, one night I go to the cinema, and the others I either study or read, or even watch television.'

'Dinner on Saturday, then,' he said firmly.

Why not? thought Kate. 'All right, I will. Thank you,' she said, and ushered him to the door.

'I'll pick you up here. About eight.' Dan looked around him. 'And by the way, leave a light on in the day to come home to, Kate. My grandmother's security needs scrutiny. I'll talk to the old man.' He leaned down suddenly and kissed her cheek. 'Goodnight, Kate.'

Kate closed the door on him and went upstairs with her flowers, oddly pleased with life and better disposed towards her homework than usual. Which, she admitted to herself, was due more to Cassie's invitation than Dan Beaumont's. She finished sooner than expected, ate a virtuously meagre supper to offset the indulgences of lunch, and was about to run her bath when the phone rang.

'Miss Harker?'

'Yes.'

'Ben Fletcher. I gather Cassie's bidden you to family lunch on Sunday. I'll pick you up just before one.'

'Please don't trouble yourself—I can walk.'

'It's a fair hike if it's raining. I'll give you a lift.'

'How kind,' said Kate coolly.

'Not in the least. And have no fear—I'll be the perfect gentleman. I saw Dan Beaumont's black eye, remember. It filled me with respect.'

'A pity it doesn't extend in other directions,' said Kate impulsively, and could have bitten her tongue.

There was a pause. 'I haven't a clue what you mean,' said Ben Fletcher rather grimly. 'I'll pick you up on Sunday.'

CHAPTER THREE

DURING the week Kate tried hard to think of some excuse to avoid lunch with the Fletchers, but in the end couldn't bring herself to lie to Cassie. At least she had Saturday night to look forward to first. Dan Beaumont was irritatingly sure of himself, but he came with impeccable references, since Mrs Beaumont was his grandmother. However, the moment she got home on Friday evening Dan rang her, his voice almost unrecognisable.

'I hoped this blasted flu would clear up,' he croaked, 'but it obviously won't before tomorrow night. I'm an aching, coughing misery. Sorry, Kate. Can we get together next week instead?'

'Of course,' Kate assured him. 'Get well soon.'

'You needn't sound *quite* so cheerful,' he complained, wheezing. 'I hoped you'd be devastated with disappointment.'

'Oh, I am, I am. I'll curl up with a good book instead.'

'That makes two of us,' said Dan bitterly, then went into a paroxysm of coughing before he gasped goodbye.

The extra Saturday staff made it an easier day for Kate, and she arrived home to find the lights blazing downstairs and Mrs Beaumont back in residence, waiting to buttonhole her about Dan's nocturnal intrusion.

'Idiot boy,' she said severely, her smile belying the words. 'Just like Dan to forget I share the house now. He should have come in during the day, not crept in at night, scaring you to death. Splendid black eye you gave him,' she added with satisfaction. 'Served him right.'

'I thought I'd killed him,' said Kate, grimacing.

'No fear. His skull's too thick,' said Mrs Beaumont, then spoiled it by saying, 'Lovable rascal, though, young Dan.'

'A very poorly one at the moment.'

'Yes. I gather he'd coaxed you to spend the evening with him. But he's caught this bug that's going round. He's gone home to mother for some tender loving care.'

'Sensible man. I shall catch up on some reading for Monday's class instead.'

'See you for coffee in the morning?' said Mrs Beaumont.

'Yes, please. Then I'm going out—bidden to lunch with Cassie Fletcher and her family. The one who writes thrillers.'

'How splendid for you, dear. You'll enjoy that.' Mrs Beaumont smiled. 'You like books so much it's a wonder you don't write a novel yourself.'

Kate was in agreement as she made supper for herself later. The incidents of this week alone would provide her with enough material, not to mention her experiences in Putney in her previous existence.

After mid-morning coffee with her landlady next day Kate went back upstairs to do rather more to her face than usual. Cassie Fletcher, pregnant or not, was one of those long-legged people who wore clothes well. When one was short of inches—vertically, anyway—dressing needed care. Kate, yearning to be ten pounds lighter, finally put on well-polished brown boots, a cream silk shirt, a full, ankle-length skirt in brown needlecord and a long waistcoat in oatmeal mohair. Her hair, thick and straight, and gleaming from its recent shampoo, she caught behind her ears with tortoiseshell barrettes and let the rest hang down her back for once. Five minutes before Ben Fletcher was due she went down to display her sartorial splendour to Mrs Beaumont, glad she was being collected when she saw that the rain was now flattening the shrubs outside in a steady downpour.

'What a day!' said Mrs Beaumont, eyeing Kate up and down. 'And what a transformation. You look lovely, my dear. What have you done to your face?'

'Gilded the lily a bit,' said Kate, smiling, then looked up as a horn hooted outside. 'That's my lift. See you later, Mrs B.'

Kate shrugged into her raincoat, collected the azalea she'd bought for Cassie and put up her umbrella to race down the path to the Range Rover backed into the cul-de-sac. As she reached it the door was flung open and a hand extended to help her up. Kate put the azalea into it, collapsed her umbrella and leapt up into the front seat unaided. Ben Fletcher put the plant on the back seat, looked at her for a moment, then said, 'Good afternoon,' with no trace of his usual smile.

'Good afternoon. Filthy day,' said Kate brightly. 'It's very good of you to collect me.'

'Not at all.' He put the vehicle into gear and nosed it out of the narrow road. 'It's not far, but in this weather you'd be drenched long before you got there.'

They continued in silence, Kate finding it impossible to think of anything to say. At this rate, she thought gloomily, the lunch party was likely to be hard work.

'Did you enjoy yourself last night?' said her companion abruptly.

Kate frowned. 'Last night?'

'Dan told me you were dining with him.'

'I was, but he's ill. Flu.'

'Really? I was away on Friday. I didn't know.'

'You work with him?'

'I work at his father's firm, yes.'

'Oh.'

'You look very different today,' he commented as they drove past the pump rooms.

'My Sunday best,' agreed Kate.

He gave her a sidelong glance. 'It's the hair. You look years younger with it down like that.'

Kate eyed him suspiciously, but he went on to discuss the weather.

'You must regret your move to Pennington when it rains like this.'

So Cassie had mentioned her transfer from London. 'It rains everywhere.'

He drew up before a tall Georgian house in a row of others of equal elegance in a square on the outskirts of the town. 'Right. Here we are. I'll get out first and put your umbrella up, then I'll come back for the plant. I assume it's for Cass?'

'Yes. It's very kind of her to invite me.'

'She likes you,' he said, in a tone which implied he felt rather differently. He leapt lightly from the vehicle, looking so good in a waxed jacket and heavy sweater, his long legs in well-worn cords, that Kate gave a little sigh, wishing he weren't quite so overpoweringly good-looking. It was hard not to respond to the sheer perfection of his face, especially now, when he was in repose, without the smile which raised her hackles so easily.

Ben Fletcher reached up and put a hand at either side of her waist to lift her down, handed her the umbrella, then reached for the azalea and locked the car. 'Right, then, Miss Harker, let's dash.'

They sprinted up the steps to the door, which opened at their approach, and a small boy hurled himself at Ben, who scooped him up, laughing. Kate raised a mental eyebrow. Ben Fletcher was obviously fond of his son.

'Quiet, you monster. Hello, Caroline; this is Kate Harker.'

A tall, fresh-faced girl shook hands with Kate. 'I help with Angus,' she said, with a friendly smile.

'And with everything else,' put in Cassie, coming along the beautiful, elegantly furnished hall. She wore a voluminous dress in finest wool the colour of almond blossom, and looked elegant despite the bulge. 'Welcome, Kate. Come on, everyone, upstairs so we can have a quiet drink before lunch. Mrs Hicks says half an hour.'

Kate handed her the plant. 'What a lovely house!'

Cassie exclaimed with pleasure over the delicate pink and white striped blossoms. 'How very sweet of you. I adore azaleas. Angus, have you said hello to Kate?'

'Hello,' said the little boy, beaming. 'I had chickenpox.'

'Goodness,' said Kate with suitable awe. 'Did you really? How nasty. I bet you itched a lot.'

Angus nodded, deeply pleased, then tugged at Ben's hand. 'Come *on*. I did painting.'

Kate, enveloped in warmth and welcome, felt oddly homesick for a moment. This might be a very impressive house, but it was also very much a home. They went upstairs and delicious scents of cooking wafted towards them on their way along the hall to what was obviously the family sitting room. No formal drawing room, this, like the room glimpsed downstairs, but a place where people read papers and books, watched television and played with Angus, whose toys were strewn all over the floor.

'Sorry about the obstacle course,' said Cassie, and went over to a drinks tray. 'What would you like? We've got the usual things, plus some rather delicious white wine.'

'A glass of that would be perfect,' said Kate, choosing a corner of a big sofa. 'What a comfortable room.'

'And messy,' chuckled Cassie. 'I work upstairs on the top floor, and leave this place to the others. Though I'm off work at the moment. Can't sit at my computer.'

'I should hope not,' said Ben, looking up from a complicated structure he was helping Angus make from plastic blocks.

'Beer, love?' said Cassie.

'Yes, but sit down. I'll get it.'

Ben uncoiled his long legs, then held out a hand to Angus. 'Come on, champ. Let's see what Mrs Hicks has made for pudding.'

When the two women were alone Cassie complimented Kate on her appearance.

'Better than the other day, then,' said Kate, grinning.

'Much better. I was rude.'

'No. I admit I don't make the best of the basic material much. So today I thought I'd make an effort. How are you and little miss Emily today?'

'She's gone a bit quiet,' admitted Cassie, shifting uncomfortably in her chair. 'Only a fortnight to go, though sometimes I wonder if she'll hang on that long. Angus arrived sooner than I thought. Still, the hospital's just up the road, thank goodness.'

Thank goodness indeed, thought Kate.

'So what's been happening in your life since I saw you last?' asked Cassie, and rather to her own surprise Kate found herself describing Dan Beaumont's break-in and her own part in it.

Cassie roared with laughter. 'Goodness, poor Dan! Ben told me he had a black eye, but I didn't realise you gave it to him.'

'It was pure fright coupled with luck,' said Kate, grinning. 'I let fly and managed to make contact.' She pulled a face. 'I thought I'd killed him at first.'

'Serves him right for creeping around at night like that,' said Cassie without sympathy, then smiled as Angus came running back into the room. 'Hello, darling; is lunch nearly ready?'

'Ten minutes,' said Angus importantly, and fixed Kate with bright blue eyes. 'Can you read?' he asked hopefully.

'What he means,' said his mother, 'is *will* you read.'

'With pleasure,' said Kate promptly. 'What story would you like?'

Angus was a handsome little boy with a mop of brown curls like his mother and bright blue eyes which shone with pleasure as he fetched a book about trains. He was dressed very simply in a sweater, jeans and small suede boots, and Kate had to restrain herself from hugging him as he sat beside her on the sofa listening to the story. Cassie sat quietly, watching them, a smile on her face. There was no sign of Ben or Caroline, and Kate lost herself in the story, suitably dramatic when the occasion demanded, her performance obviously meeting with approval as Angus drank in every word. When the story finished he thanked Kate without being prompted, then looked at his mother.

'Is it ten minutes, Mummy?'

Cassie consulted her watch. 'Oh, yes. It is. Will you run upstairs and call Daddy?'

Angus nodded happily and scampered off, then Caroline popped her head round the door.

'First course ready and waiting, ladies.'

'Right you are, Caro. Give me time to heave myself up.'

Kate leapt to give Cassie a hand, then followed her from the room to a dining room. The table was laid for five with gleaming crystal and silverware and a flat centrepiece of miniature daffodils and freesias.

Caroline cast a glance over the table, checked the soup tureen on the hotplate at the end of the sideboard, then smiled at Cassie. 'Right, then, I'll be off now. See you in the morning. I'll get my kiss from Angus on the way out.'

'Enjoy yourself,' said Cassie, then looked up with a smile as a tall, dark man entered the room with Angus. 'Hello, darling; finished your paper? This is Kate Harker, the lady who organised my signing session the other week. Kate, this is my husband.'

'Alec Neville,' said the distinguished newcomer, shaking hands with Kate. 'I gather you're new to Pennington. Thank you for looking after my wife. I had to get Ben to deputise for me that day. I was operating.'

'Alec's a plastic surgeon,' explained Cassie to a temporarily speechless Kate. 'Angus, can you find your uncle, please? Tell him lunch is ready. Alec, will you open more wine?'

*   *   *

Kate ate delicious vegetable soup in a daze, trying to pull herself together and behave like a guest. One who might even be asked to visit this delightful household again if she was very, very lucky. Angus was seated between his parents, Ben next to Cassie, and Kate next to Alec Neville, who was an attractive man in his mid-forties and very obviously devoted to his wife. Cassie gave Kate a few searching glances, but once they'd embarked on the roast, and Mrs Hicks, the cheerful cook, had been paid sincere compliments and bidden an affectionate goodbye before she went off for the day, Kate had come to terms with her mistake and was able to contribute to the conversation.

Both men were amused when Cassie told how Dan Beaumont got his black eye.

'So that's the story,' said Ben with a grin. 'He refused to say why he got it.'

Kate pulled a face. 'I shouldn't have mentioned it, I suppose.'

'It won't do his ego any harm to admit he was clobbered by a girl—and a small one at that,' said Alec, chuckling. 'Young Dan's a shade too full of himself. Always had it easy, with a job ready and waiting for him at the family firm.'

'Oh, I don't know, Alec,' said Ben, helping himself to more roast potatoes. 'To be fair, Dan's a damned good marketing man. His father's not into sinecures. He hires the best man for the job.'

'Obviously,' said Cassie, smiling at him affectionately. 'After all he promoted you to technical director of the firm. No mean feat at your age. Eat your cabbage, Angus. See, Ben's eaten all his.'

The little boy spooned up the rest of his lunch, then smiled seraphically. 'Pudding, please.'

Cassie half rose, but Ben leapt to his feet. 'Stay put, Cass. Mrs Hicks showed me where everything is.'

'May I help?' asked Kate as Alec rose to collect the plates.

'By all means.' He gave her a warm smile. 'Normally we see to ourselves on weekends, but now Cassie's near her time Caroline and Mrs Hicks insist on doing a bit extra until the baby arrives—and probably for a while afterwards too.'

Kate collected the used china and silver from the main course and stacked plates and tureens on a large tray Mrs Hicks had left on the sideboard, but Alec hefted it to take it to the kitchen. 'Thank you, Kate. Now stay and talk to Cassie while Ben and I forage for the next bit. Angus, you can come to the kitchen with me and tell me what you want for pudding.'

'He'll choose ice-cream,' said Cassie, smiling as she watched them go.

'You didn't eat much,' said Kate anxiously. 'Are you all right?'

'I just don't have room these days. I eat a bit now and then, rather than a full meal. Though I'm determined to have some apricot tart. Mrs Hicks is a genius with pastry.' Cassie fixed her guest with a challenging brown gaze. 'Now, then, Kate Harker, tell me what shattered you so much when Alec appeared.'

Kate sighed. She'd hoped Cassie hadn't noticed. 'I feel such a fool.'

'Why?'

Kate looked her hostess in the eye. 'When you came to the signing I thought Ben was your husband. I'm new around here, remember. No one thought to tell me he was your brother.'

Cassie stared for a moment, then dissolved into helpless laughter. 'So that's why Ben thought you disliked him! He wasn't keen to come to lunch today when he heard you'd been invited.'

'I'm not surprised,' said Kate glumly. 'I almost didn't come myself. Because I saw him with Gail.'

'Gail?'

'The junior bookseller at Hardacres.'

'The girl with the long blonde hair?' Cassie gurgled. 'Oh, dear. Ben's such a menace—can't resist a pretty face.'

'I saw them having lunch together that day after he'd taken you home—'

'And thought the toyboy husband was having it off with a cute little bimbo while his poor pregnant wife went home to their son. Oh, dear, oh, dear.' Cassie mopped her eyes. 'I'm sorry, Kate, it's my fault. Ben's so well-known in Pennington I never even thought to say he was my little brother. Well, not little, exactly, but eight years younger than me. When Alec's tied up he tends to rope him in to keep an eye on me at the moment. Ben and I have always been close.'

'I'd better apologise, I suppose,' said Kate uncomfortably.

'What for? You haven't done anything.' Cassie leaned across the table and patted her hand. 'Leave it, Kate. Girls tend to throw themselves at our Benedict because he's so good-looking. Do him good to meet one impervious to the Fletcher charm for a change.'

The two men returned, Ben carrying a dish of ice-cream for Angus in one hand and a platter of cheeses in the other. Alec deposited a large apricot tart in front of Cassie, took a jug of cream from the sideboard, then resumed his seat by Kate.

Consigning her diet to the winds, Kate accepted the slice of tart Cassie cut for her, and helped herself to cream.

'What were you laughing about in here?' demanded Ben as he settled Angus in his chair.

'Girl stuff,' said Cassie serenely. 'Tart or cheese, Ben?'

Kate ate her tart with enjoyment, feeling a lot happier now her mistake over Ben Fletcher had been explained to her. It had bothered her that a clever, charming woman like Cassie was seemingly married to a rotter. Not, of course, that Ben Fletcher *was* a rotter. He was free to chat up as many willing females as he liked. And Alec Neville was a very fitting mate for Cassie—a sophisticated man who obviously adored his wife and son.

Euphoric at the discovery, Kate joined in the general conversation with enthusiasm, discussing the current play at the repertory theatre, listening to an account of the paper Alec was writing to give at a medical dinner, and contributing anecdotes of her own about some of the authors encountered at the Kensington branch of Hardacres.

'What made you leave London for quiet old Pennington?' asked Ben.

She had the answer off pat by this time. 'Promotion.'

'And how do you like it here?' asked Alec, taking his son on his knee.

Kate smiled at the sleepy little boy. 'Very much. I missed some things when I first came here. But there are more pros than cons now I'm settling in.'

'I gather old Mrs Beaumont is your landlady,' said Alec. 'I operated on her hand years ago. How is she?'

'Arthritic, but otherwise bright as a button. We get on well.'

'It must be nice for her to have someone young in the house,' said Cassie. 'Alec, will you take Angus up for a nap?'

'I will. And then I'm going to polish up my deathless prose until he wakes.'

'I must be going—' began Kate.

'Please don't,' said Cassie. 'Stay and chat for a while. Ben's probably off to the gym for a bit. He'll come back and drive you home after tea.'

'Oh, please don't bother,' said Kate promptly, avoiding Ben's eye. 'I can walk home—'

'No bother,' said Ben, getting up. 'I'm coming back for tea anyway. See you later. Thanks for the lunch, Cassie. I don't know what Mrs Hicks does to roast beef, but she's a genius. Do you think she'd marry me?'

'Over my dead body,' said Alec promptly, hoisting his sleeping son. 'Send one of your girlfriends on a cookery course.'

'They're all on diets,' Ben sighed. 'Low-fat everything and designer lettuce.'

Kate let out a giggle, and he raised an eyebrow at her, said he'd be back at five, brushed a hand over Angus's curls and strolled from the room.

'Couldn't I wash up or something?' said Kate, when Cassie was settled in the sitting room with a cushion in the small of her back.

'Certainly not. It's all in the dishwasher. Just pour me my daily ration of coffee, and talk to me while we have the chance. Angus won't sleep long. He'll be back in an hour, wanting a playmate, I warn you.'

Kate chuckled. 'I don't mind.'

'You like children?'

'I don't know any. My sister's older than me, and married, but no family yet. And none of my friends have offspring to date.'

'Would you like some yourself?'

Kate thought about it. 'Yes. In time. But I want to do things with my life first.'

'Don't leave it too long. I nearly did.' Cassie paused, her eyes absent. 'Alec and I knew each other when we were young, but I sent him away and ten years of our lives were lost to us. Still,' she added philosophically, 'if I hadn't I might never have started writing.'

'Which would have been a shame!' Kate leaned forward to refill their coffee-cups. 'But why did you choose crime?'

Cassie explained about her job in a pathology laboratory, which had led to an acquaintance with a Detective Inspector in the local CID. 'So there it was, all at hand, so to speak.'

Kate listened with avid interest as Cassie explained how she constructed her plots and the relationship between her main characters, the time passing so quickly that Alec returned with Angus all too soon. But Kate enjoyed herself just as much as she helped the little boy build an airport while his father went back to polish up his lecture. A little later Cassie went off to the bathroom, then came back, pausing in the doorway.

'Kate,' she said quietly.

'Yes?' Kate looked up to see Cassie breathing deeply and got quietly to her feet, instinct telling her what was happening. 'The baby?'

'Yes. Would you fetch Alec? Upstairs, first on the right.' She smiled valiantly.

'Come on, Angus,' said Kate, holding out her hand. 'Will you show me where Daddy is, please?'

The little boy nodded importantly, and led the way up to the study at the top of the house, where Alec was deep in a sheaf of papers.

'It's Cassie,' said Kate as Alec looked up in enquiry then leapt to his feet at the look on her face.

'Right!' He went ahead of them, taking the stairs two at a time, Kate following more slowly, holding Angus by the hand.

In the sitting room Cassie bent to hug her little son. 'Darling, will you be a good boy and stay with Kate while Daddy and Mummy go to the hospital to get your new baby sister?' She gave Kate an apologetic look. 'Sorry to throw you in at the deep end, but if you could just hang on here until Ben gets back? Or ring him at the gym.'

'We'll be fine,' said Kate, hoping this was true. Alec came in, suitcase in hand, wrapped his wife in a raincoat, gave Angus a swift hug and told him he'd be back later, then smiled appreciatively at Kate.

'We're very grateful—thanks a lot. Come on, my darling, gently does it.'

Kate took Angus down to the front door to wave his parents off in the Daimler parked ready at the kerb, then climbed back upstairs, hoping her lack of experience with children wasn't too obvious to Angus, who'd looked a little forlorn as the car took his parents away.

'Ben's coming to tea,' he announced as they settled on the floor again in a welter of building blocks.

'Good. What do you like best for tea?'

'Ice-cream!'

Again? thought Kate with misgiving.

'And beans,' added Angus.

'On toast?'

He nodded, and Kate felt happier. Beans on toast was well within her scope. They had a happy time together for a while, building a garage, before Angus tired of construction work.

'*Aladdin*, please,' he said.

Kate made for the pile of books, but Angus shook his head impatiently. He trotted over to the cupboard below the television, took out a video and handed it to Kate. She heaved a sigh of relief, started the video playing, and they settled down together on the sofa to watch the animated antics of the cartoon fairy tale. Angus chortled happily at the genie, so immersed in the magic that he didn't see Ben when his uncle appeared in the doorway.

'Where's everybody?' enquired Ben, and Angus shot to his feet, rushing to his tall uncle.

'Mummy's gone to get the baby!' he cried, and hurled himself into the strong, familiar arms. Ben met Kate's eyes over the curly head.

'Long?' he asked.

'About an hour.'

'Lucky you were here!'

'Only too glad to help.'

'Come and watch *Aladdin*!' demanded Angus, then added, 'Please,' at Ben's look.

'Right.'

'Kate too,' said the child, and, feeling extraordinarily flattered that he wanted her there, Kate sat on the sofa next to Angus, with Ben on the other side.

'Do you need to get home?' asked Ben in an undertone, catching her eye.

Kate shook her head.

'Then will you stay for a while? Until bedtime for this chap, if necessary?'

'Of course. I'd be glad to.' She smiled. 'Angus fancies beans on toast for his supper. I could do that if you'd direct me to the kitchen.'

'No hurry. When he's had enough of this we'll all go and put tea together. OK with you, Angus?'

'OK,' agreed Angus absently, his attention on the genie.

CHAPTER FOUR

'THIS must be rather different from your usual Sundays,' said Ben as he led Kate to the kitchen. It was a pleasant place, with a black and white checkered floor and copper pans hanging from hooks. He took a stainless-steel pan from a cupboard. 'Use this for the beans. The others are window-dressing.'

'My usual Sundays are rather different,' said Kate drily. 'Salad for lunch and homework all afternoon, followed by television or reading in the evening. Today wins by miles for entertainment value.'

He grinned. 'I thought Cass was a bit ambitious, entertaining a guest for lunch at this stage, but in the event it was a stroke of genius—ready-made company for Angus and me.'

'You could have coped on your own.'

'But it's better for Angus. Having someone new on hand is diverting him from the situation.'

Angus drew busily at the kitchen table while they prepared the meal. Kate looked at him, smiling, then stirred the beans, cut the toast into fingers and served the little boy his supper.

'You're used to children?' asked Ben as he sat down at the table.

'No. That's how I like *my* beans on toast.'

He looked thoughtful. 'Beans and salad. Is that all you eat?'

Her lips twitched. 'No. I eat low-fat things too—with lashings of designer lettuce, of course.'

He laughed, his eyes dancing, and suddenly Kate felt the full candlepower of a charm so effortless that its owner had no idea of its effect. 'Ouch! I obviously touched a nerve there.' He frowned, his eyes moving over her. 'But surely you don't need to keep to that kind of thing?'

'I'm trying to lose ten pounds,' she admitted frankly.

'What the hell for?' His surprise was as genuine as it was flattering. 'Most men go for curves.'

'My diet is to please me, not a man,' she assured him tartly.

Ben looked unconvinced. 'Why do you want to be thinner?'

'I used to share a flat with three other girls, all of whom were at least eight inches taller and several pounds lighter than me. I developed a fixation.' Kate got up and took Angus's plate. 'Right. What now, darling?'

'Ice-cream?' he said hopefully.

Kate raised her eyebrows at Ben, who shrugged and took a carton of vanilla ice-cream from the freezer and spooned some into a dish.

'Want a banana with it, Angus?'

'After, please.' Angus demolished the ice-cream, then, true to his word, disposed of a banana while Ben went off to answer the telephone.

When he came back his face was carefully blank. 'That was Daddy, Angus. Would you mind if Kate and I put you to bed tonight? Mummy's still waiting for the baby, and she wants Daddy to wait with her.'

Angus's lower lip wobbled for a moment, then he blinked manfully. 'OK, then. Mummy reads me lots of stories,' he added, fixing Kate with a cajoling blue gaze.

'Then so will I,' she promised, smiling warmly. 'Er, could I visit a bathroom, please, gentlemen?'

Ben took Angus by the hand. 'You go and collect up the books while I show Kate where to go.' Once the child had trotted along the hall to the sitting room Ben bent to talk in Kate's ear.

'Looks like being a long haul. Miss Neville's in no hurry. Alec sounded a bit stressed, asked if I could sleep here tonight in case he doesn't make it home.'

'Problems?' asked Kate anxiously.

'Cassie was a long time producing Angus,' he said evasively. 'I hope to God she's all right.' He squared his impressive shoulders. 'Anyway I must ring my mother and tell her what's happening, then contact Alec's secretary and cancel his list for tomorrow.'

'What can I do to help?'

'You could stay here for a bit if you would.' He smiled crookedly. 'I could do with some moral support.'

'Right. It's my day off tomorrow, so it doesn't matter if I'm home late.' She smiled reassuringly. 'Give me a minute, then I'll come and help with bathtime if you like.'

'I like very much. Thank you.'

Glad of a few minutes to herself in the bathroom, Kate tidied her hair, renewed her lipstick, then went back to the others to find Angus insisting it was too early yet for bed. Since neither adult felt like risking an upset, they both settled to helping the child with some puzzles, then they watched more of the *Aladdin* video, by which time Angus was heavy-eyed and agreeable to a bath.

Bathtime with a little one was a new experience for Kate, but obviously not for Ben. He was surprisingly adept as he undressed his little nephew and tested the temperature of the bathwater. Angus launched a flotilla of little boats into the water from the side of the bath, and there was much racing and splashing through bubbles before the little boy consented to come out into the warm towel Kate was holding. She wrapped him up and cuddled him to her, glad to see that his eyes were even heavier now. It would be better for Angus if he slept the anxious hours away until his little sister arrived.

'Right, then,' she said briskly as she helped him put on his pyjamas. 'Have you decided which books you want?'

By the time Kate had read herself hoarse the little boy was almost asleep, and Angus made no objection when Ben scooped him up at last and tucked him into bed in the small room next to his parents' bedroom. Angus settled down, then looked up at his tall uncle. 'I miss Mummy,' he quavered.

'I know you do, old chap,' said Ben, kneeling beside the bed. 'But she'll be home soon—Daddy too. And to-morrow Grandma and Mike will be here. So be a brave lad and settle down to sleep. I'm staying here tonight, by the way,' he added reassuringly.

'Are you?' Angus gave his uncle a delighted smile, yawned widely, let Kate give him a kiss, then closed his eyes and snuggled down in the bed.

'I'll sit here for a while,' said Ben softly, and Kate nodded, then went downstairs to collect building blocks and put toys away in a large chest.

When Ben joined her she was sitting in a corner of the sofa trying to interest herself in the Sunday papers.

'It's an hour later than his usual time,' he said, yawning, 'but I don't suppose it matters.' He looked at his watch. 'I wish Alec would ring. Which reminds me, I must do my telephoning. Excuse me for a minute.'

Kate nodded, wondering what to do next. It was almost eight o'clock and still no word from the hospital. Four hours. Surely the baby ought to arrive soon? Not that she knew much about it. Poor Cassie, in pain all this time. And maybe for hours more yet. Kate pulled a face. It was a pity there wasn't some other way of achieving the miracle.

Ben came in, looking haggard, and sat down. 'Mother's philosophical. Apparently it took a long time for Cassie and me to come into the world too. I thought it might be quicker these days, somehow. I spoke to Margaret, Alec's secretary, so she'll organise everything for him. She suggested I get Caroline back tonight, but it seems a shame to spoil her time with her bloke. He's on leave from the army and goes back tomorrow.'

'Then leave her in peace. Angus is in bed, and if he wakes you're here, which is the next best thing to his parents,' said Kate.

'And you're here too, lucky for Angus—and for me.' He smiled ruefully. 'I hope you're not sorry you came to lunch with Cassie.'

Kate smiled cheerfully. 'Absolutely not. And if it's any help to you I'm willing to stay as long as you like. Feel free to say if you'd rather I went, though. I'll quite understand—'

'Hell, no,' said Ben fervently. 'I appreciate the company.'

Kate looked him in the eye. 'I just thought there might be someone else you could ask round.'

He returned the look in kind. 'As it happens there isn't. No one who would make beans on toast and let Angus soak her through at bathtime, anyway. Most of my female acquaintances tend to the decorative rather than the practical.'

'Why?' said Kate bluntly. 'Is a pretty face an essential requirement?'

His eyes narrowed. 'No.' He paused, then shrugged. 'Look, when I first went to college I was just like any other bloke fresh from a single-sex school—like a kid let loose in the sweetie shop. But these days, despite my totally undeserved reputation, women feature in only a small part of my life. I like my work, spend a fair amount of social time with my male colleagues, or working out at a gym, and for home comforts I come here or go on a trip to Wales to see my mother. The odd pretty face to kiss and—er—wine and dine is all I need for the time being.'

He paused again, his dark eyes gleaming below the expensively cut gilt hair. 'Tell me the truth, Kate Harker. You thought I was Cassie's husband, didn't you? I could feel laser beams of disapproval the moment we met again at Hardacres.'

For the first time in years Kate blushed to the roots of her hair. 'Yes,' she said baldly, 'I did.'

'And looked down your nose at me because I'm years younger than she is.'

'It would be very difficult for me to look *down* my nose at you,' Kate pointed out. 'But you're right. I did disapprove. Not because of the difference in age, though.'

'Then why?'

'Gail.'

'Ah.' He nodded slowly. 'You thought Cassie's husband was seducing an innocent young maiden right under his pregnant wife's nose.'

Kate nodded. 'Exactly.'

'So why didn't you tell Cassie the day you lunched together?'

'None of my business.'

'Gail, then. She works for you.'

'What she does out of working hours is her own affair.'

'Yet you still accepted the invitation to lunch today,' he went on relentlessly. 'Why?'

'Because I like your sister more than anyone I've met in a long time.' Kate's smile was mocking. 'If your company was the price to pay for an hour or two in Cassie's it seemed worth it.'

'Thanks! But now you know I'm her brother, do you feel more kindly disposed towards me?' he demanded.

Kate looked at him steadily. He was leaning back in a big leather chair, his endless legs stretched straight out in front of him, relaxed and self-confident and, she fancied, prepared to exert his considerable charm to bring her to heel. 'Yes, it's a great relief to know Cassie's married to a mature, attractive man who obviously adores her, instead of to a—'

'Two-timing gigolo years younger than herself?'

'Right.'

'Are you glad I'm not married to anyone?'

'Yes, very,' said Kate sweetly. 'For Gail's sake.'

He leaned forward suddenly. 'Look, Kate, Gail was someone I took out for a meal one night. Nothing more. She's a nice kid, and very sweet, but to be frank it was a pretty boring evening. I took her home, thanked her nicely, and that was it. I didn't even kiss her.'

Kate shook her head disapprovingly. 'Poor Gail. Choose someone your own size next time.'

'Few women are.'

'You know what I mean,' she said crossly, then looked up in alarm as a cry came from upstairs, and with one accord they both bolted from the room to see to Angus.

The little boy was sitting up in bed, crying, his eyes piteous as he reached out to Ben. 'I want my mummy,' he sobbed. Ben held him close, murmuring to him softly, his long hand smoothing the brown curls.

'There, there, old chap. Mummy's not home yet. She's still waiting for the baby. But Daddy rang and asked if you were a good boy. I told him you were a cracker— ate the supper Kate made for you and went off to bed like a real champion.'

Angus peeped over Ben's shoulder at Kate. 'Story?' he said hoarsely.

Kate looked at Ben for approval, then nodded, smiling. 'All right, darling.'

'Drink too?' asked the child.

'OK,' said Ben. 'But let's take a hike to the bathroom first.'

Ben brought Angus back, then went off for orange juice. Kate sat down on the chair by the bed and took Angus on her knee, holding him close as she read to him from a book of fairy tales. *Puss in Boots* met with approval, and at first she read with drama, then gradually made her voice more and more monotonous as the child's lids began to close. By the time Ben came back Angus was asleep again. He took the little boy from her, laid him down gently, pulled the covers over him, then tiptoed from the room with Kate.

'I hope that doesn't happen too often tonight,' said Ben fervently, and eyed Kate in appeal. 'Look, I know it's a lot to ask, but Angus has obviously taken a fancy to you, and if he wakes wanting his mother again I have a nasty feeling I won't do. Could you possibly stay here tonight?'

'Yes, of course I will,' said Kate promptly. 'But I'd better ring Mrs Beaumont to tell her. She might worry if I don't come home at all tonight.'

'Not a practice of yours, I take it.'

'No, it certainly isn't.'

Mrs Beaumont was very grateful for Kate's consideration, though Kate's explanation was brief, to keep the line free.

'Are you hungry?' asked Ben when she rejoined him.

'Does that mean you are?'

He grinned. 'Bull's-eye! Let's make some sandwiches. There must be roast beef left over from lunch, and there's a telephone extension in the kitchen.'

It was a relief to have something to do. Kate buttered bread while Ben sliced roast beef and showed her where to find horseradish sauce and mustard.

They sat in the kitchen, a platter of sandwiches between them, and were halfway through the meal when Alec rang again.

Kate tensed as Ben listened, reassured Alec that his son was sleeping, then put the phone down and heaved a worried sigh.

'She's still in labour. Alec says she's doing marvellously—better than Alec by the sound of it.'

'Perhaps it's worse for him than for other fathers—because he's a doctor, I mean.'

'True. Have another sandwich.'

'I don't think I can,' Kate sighed, her appetite suddenly gone.

'No. Neither can I.' Ben's jaw clenched. 'I wish Cass would get on with it. I hate to think of her—'

'Then don't,' said Kate firmly. 'Come on. Let's find a film to watch on television, or play Scrabble or something.'

To her surprise Ben opted for Scrabble with some enthusiasm. 'Haven't played for years, though; I'm pretty rusty.' He grinned. 'It's not the way I pass time with a girl as a rule.'

'Nice change for you, then,' said Kate, and set out the board while Ben went up to check on Angus.

'Out for the count,' he reported when he came back. 'Fancy a drink, Kate?'

She shook her head. 'I'll make some coffee later.'

'Good idea. Keep us awake.'

'Somehow I don't think that'll be a problem!'

'True. How much do I score for "zoo"?'

Unsurprised to find Ben a highly competitive player, Kate enjoyed the game very much. Angus remained quiet, and for a while Ben's fierce concentration diverted him from his anxiety over his sister. But after a second game Ben suggested they make coffee and just talk.

He smiled. 'Do a Scheherazade for me, tell me stories.'

'Fairy tales?' said Kate drily as they went off to the kitchen.

'No. Non-fiction, please. The Kate Harker story.' He started up the coffee-maker, then leaned against the counter, smiling encouragingly. 'Tell me why you exchanged metropolitan delights for Pennington.'

'I told you. Promotion.'

'I heard you. But I fancy there's more to it than that. Come clean, Kate. Man trouble?'

Her eyes flashed. 'I should have known you'd think that.'

Ben shook his head. 'Actually I didn't until today.'

She put mugs and milk and sugar on a tray, then threw a frowning look over her shoulder. 'What do you mean?'

Ben leaned against the counter again. 'No book-ends here so I hope I'm safe from attack if I say that at Hardacres, with your hair screwed up and those horn-rimmed glasses, not to mention the icy disapproval, you didn't come across as a sexpot exactly. But today, with your hair down and a spot of warpaint, it's different. I can see what Dan meant.'

'Dan?' said Kate, stiffening.

'He said his grandmother had this terrific girl as a lodger. Yards of dark hair and huge black eyes—'

'Dilated with terror, to be accurate,' said Kate tartly. 'It was Dan who got the black eye. Mine are grey. Is that coffee ready?'

Ben put the pot on the tray and carried it to the door. 'After you.'

'Shall I just run up and peep at Angus?'

Angus, Kate was glad to see, was fast asleep. She pulled the covers higher, stood looking at him for a moment, then went back down to find Ben watching the news on television. He jumped to his feet and switched off the set, eyebrows raised in query.

'Fast asleep,' Kate assured him.

'I wonder for how long!'

'Have some coffee.'

They sat in opposite corners of the sofa, sipping the strong, dark brew in silence for a while, then Ben put his mug on the tray and sat back.

'Come on, then, Scheherazade, entertain me. Tell me about this man trouble.'

Kate frowned. 'Why do you want to know?'

He smiled. 'If you're nursing a broken heart I'm your man. I'm good at mending things.'

She chuckled. 'Sorry to disappoint you. Heart all in one piece. Mine, anyway.'

'Ah. You did the heartbreaking.'

'Wrong again.'

'Curiouser and curiouser. Explain,' he commanded, settling lower in his corner.

Kate finished her coffee. 'Oh, very well. But I warn you, it's pretty boring stuff.'

'I'm sure it's not. Go on,' he encouraged. 'You know how stories start. I heard you tonight with Angus.'

She laughed. 'Oh, I see. Once upon a time, then, there were four girls who went to the same university, and afterwards shared a flat while they hunted for jobs and embarked on various careers.'

Kate and Ally, she revealed, had been at school together before college. Liz and Emma formed the rest of the quartet, and they all got on together remarkably well. Ally worked in a bank, Liz for one of the large Sunday papers, Emma was something lowly with an independent television company, and Kate, of course, worked at Hardacres.

'So what went wrong?' asked Ben.

'Nothing much did for years. We all had boyfriends, some of us more than others. Emma in particular usually did a balancing act with at least three men at once. Liz and I had one or two male friends we went out with on a casual sort of basis, but a few months before this tale really gets going, Ally, the quiet one, met the love of her life and started talking wedding bells.'

'Did you ever get in each other's way, with all these guys hanging round?'

'Oh, yes. But I often went home to Guildford at the weekend, and Emma and Liz would sometimes stay over with whoever they were romancing at the time, so Ally usually had the flat to herself on Sundays. Then suddenly Ally began to get temperamental and tearful.'

'Her lover not as true as she'd thought?' asked Ben drily.

Kate nodded. 'Nicholas told her she was imagining things, that he'd never looked at another girl. He made a speech in front of us all, the pig, and Ally was happy again. But not for long.'

One night, Kate went on to explain, she had arrived home weary and footsore from a late shift at the bookstore and found herself confronted by a raging, hysterical Ally. She'd accused Kate of wrecking her life, hurled epithets which had made Kate lose her temper at last. But nothing would convince Ally that Kate wasn't the 'poisonous slag' who'd stolen Nicholas. She could have understood it, she'd shrieked, if it had been Liz or Emma, but not an overweight little frump like Kate.

'Nice girl!' said Ben with distaste. 'What was he like, this Nicholas?'

'Tall, darkish, good-looking in a bland sort of way. Something in the City. You know the type. And Ally's a nice girl, but more an English rose than a sexpot.' Kate sighed. 'Anyway, Emma was the culprit. She's a sexy redhead who just can't resist making up to a man, and

in spite of the stuffed-shirt image Nick's a normal chap
with a full set of hormones. You can guess the rest.'

'End of quartet.'

'Yes. Nick did a runner, I jumped at the job here in
Pennington, Emma and Liz found a new flat together,
and Ally went home to her parents.'

'Did she apologise to you?'

'More or less. But things won't ever be the same between us.' Kate shrugged. 'A pity, but life goes on.'

'And the men friends you left behind—do you still
see any of them?'

'No. When I came here I made a clean break. Ally
hurt me a lot—we'd known each other since we were
children, remember. Her crowning insult stuck in my
mind like glue. But I keep in touch with Emma and Liz,'
she added.

'No hard feelings towards Emma?'

'No. It takes two. Nick could have told her to get lost.
And if he's that easy to seduce from the straight and
narrow it's as well Ally found out before she married
him, not after.'

'So you require a high standard from men who come
courting, Kate Harker!'

'If you mean I'd prefer a man who didn't leap into
bed with my friends, yes,' said Kate lightly. 'But for the
time being having a life to myself is so restful, the subject
doesn't arise.' She fixed him with an expectant eye.
'Right. That's enough about me. Now it's your turn.'

CHAPTER FIVE

BEN responded with a sketch of his work on computer software at Beaumont Electronics, told her about his mother and stepfather and their seaside home in Wales, then Angus woke in distress and it took the best part of an hour and the concerted efforts of both Kate and Ben to settle him down again.

They made more coffee and returned to the sitting room, both of them heavy-eyed and weary, Ben making very little effort by this time to hide the anxiety that was etching haggard lines into his handsome face. When the phone rang at just after two he leapt up to answer it, his face quickly alight with such relief and joy that Kate, close behind him, sagged against the wall, limp with reaction.

'Emily Catherine born twenty minutes ago, seven and a half pounds, and Cassie's all right,' he said in one breath, then seized Kate by the elbows, lifted her high in the air and whirled her round.

'Put me down, you idiot!' she gasped, laughing, and Ben gave her a smacking kiss on both cheeks, rubbed noses with her, then set her on her feet and gave a great, uninhibited yawn.

'Alec will be back as soon as he can.' He thrust the bright hair back from his forehead. 'I could take you home, if you like. Caroline will be here at eight in the morning to see to Angus and take him off to nursery school, so Alec can probably lie in for a bit now his list for the day is cancelled.'

'Good idea,' said Kate approvingly. 'I quite fancy a lie-in myself. I suddenly feel very weary.'

'Ditto,' he agreed. 'Perhaps I'll get in a bit later for once too.'

When Alec Neville finally arrived he had great dark marks under eyes blazing with elation.

'Your sister's a star,' he said to Ben, clapping him on the shoulder. 'I wanted her to have a Caesarian section, but while there was a chance of delivering naturally she stuck it out, determined to carry on.'

Kate retreated, feeling distinctly shy now she was no longer needed, but Ben reached out a long arm to take her by the hand and draw her close. 'Thank God I had Kate here to lend a hand. Angus woke up a few times wanting his mummy, and Kate was a better substitute than me.'

'You didn't know what you were letting yourself in for when you said yes to lunch with us, Kate,' said Alec, smiling. 'I can't thank you enough for helping out. I thought we had almost three weeks to go, but Emily was in a hurry.'

'I was only too glad there was something I could do,' Kate assured him. 'But you must be tired. Ben's going to drive me home now—'

'Not yet!' said Alec. 'You must toast my daughter first. I've had some champagne on ice for the last week.'

Kate made more beef sandwiches while she drank her champagne, since Alec found he was starving now the strain of the past few hours was over.

'I was just about climbing the wall by the time you rang,' said Ben with feeling. 'I was sure something was wrong.'

'I didn't enjoy the last hour myself,' said Alec with a shudder. 'It's the one time when a man is entirely helpless to do anything for his wife other than hold her hand and just be there for her. Only in my case I kept picturing the things that could go wrong—'

'But Cassie's all right, Alec?' said Ben in sudden alarm.

'Absolutely. When I left her she was fast asleep—so was Emily. You can visit them tomorrow. You too, Kate.'

Kate flushed. 'Oh, but your wife won't want—'

'She particularly asked you to. Both Kates, she said.'

Ben grinned. 'The other Kate's my mother. She'll have Mike, my stepfather, on the road at first light.'

Half an hour later Ben drew the Range Rover up outside Waverley Lodge and switched off the ignition. 'Right, then, Kate Harker. Three in the morning and all's well. What a day!'

Kate hesitated. 'I'm very glad I was part of it. You were all very welcoming to the stranger in your midst—'

'You're not a stranger now!'

'Thank you. I'm glad.'

'It's I who should be thanking you, Kate.' Ben leaned over and kissed her on the cheek. 'Goodnight. Sleep well. I'll call for you about seven tomorrow.' He opened his door and came round the car to lift her down, then stood looking down at her face by the light of the streetlamp. He gave her an odd, crooked smile, brushed his hand over her hair, then stepped back.

'Goodnight, Ben. Thank you for driving me home,' she said breathlessly, and turned away to hurry up the short garden path. She unlocked the door and turned to wave at Ben, who stood waiting under the lamp, his hair gleaming. He raised a hand in reply, then Kate shut the door quietly and crept up the stairs in the dark.

She was in bed when it suddenly struck her that she couldn't visit Cassie the following night after all. She was due at her evening class.

Next day, after giving Mrs Beaumont the glad tidings, Kate walked into town and bought a cuddly pink bunny for the baby, a toy car for Angus, so that he wouldn't feel left out, then went to the florist's and asked them to send a posy of spring flowers to Cassie, with the simple message 'Love, Kate' attached. Then she looked up the number of Beaumont Electronics and phoned Ben from a callbox. When she asked to be put through to Mr Fletcher's extension a hoarse, familiar voice said, 'Beaumont here.'

'Dan?' said Kate, surprised. 'This is Kate Harker. I was trying to contact Ben Fletcher. Are you better?'

'No,' he said gloomily. 'But that cuts no ice with my father. Anyway, why do you want Ben? He's in a meeting right now.'

Kate hesitated. 'I see. Could you leave him a message? Say I can't make it tonight. I'd forgotten my evening class, and I'm too near my exam to miss it. Would you ask him to ring me to arrange another time?'

'Well, well, you're a dark horse, Kate! All right. Leave it to me.'

'Thanks, Dan. Bye.'

When Kate got home from her evening class that night Mrs Beaumont came out into the hall.

'Hello, dear. You had a telephone call from Mrs Neville, thanking you for the flowers. She's sorry you couldn't make it tonight and wondered if you might find time to visit her tomorrow.'

'Thanks, Mrs B. Goodnight.'

Kate was so weary after her missed sleep that she rushed through a bath and fell into bed with a towel over her pillow, too tired to dry her hair first. She still felt tired when she arrived at the shop the next morning, but the familiar routine soon took over and at one point she informed her staff that she was adding an hour off to her lunch-break and would leave at twelve and be back by two.

'My first rep's not due until two-thirty,' she reported to Mrs Harrison.

'Of course, Kate. Something important?'

'A hospital visit. Mrs Neville—Quinn Fletcher—gave birth to a daughter yesterday. She's asked me to pop in to see her.'

Everyone sent their best wishes when they heard where Kate was going, feeling a proprietorial interest in Quinn Fletcher's baby, though Gail looked positively tragic as she added hers. Ben had done well to nip Gail's interest in the bud, thought Kate, then frowned. Was she making excuses for him, by any chance? If so she could stop that right away. Circumstances had thrown them together in a particularly emotive way, it was true, but there was no reason to lose her head over him herself. In the un-likely event of a relationship with him they'd make an ill-assorted pair, she thought, with a twisted little smile. Ben was so overpoweringly handsome. And although Kate was a little less rounded than in her London days she had no illusions about herself. Most of the time Ally's insult was a cap that fitted rather too well.

Kate took a taxi to the hospital, and was shown into the private wing where Cassie Neville was sitting up in bed, reading, her baby daughter in a cot by her side.

'Hello, Cassie,' said Kate rather shyly.

'Kate!' Cassie threw down her book and held out her hands. 'How lovely to see you. I didn't expect you at this time of day. Are you playing hookey?'

Kate's throat thickened as Cassie gave her an affectionate hug. 'I took time off. I brought something for Emily—and for Angus, too. Will you tell him it's from Kate with love?'

'How very thoughtful of you.' Cassie beamed. 'Thank you. He'll love it. Now let me introduce you to my daughter.'

Kate hung over the cot, almost afraid to breathe as she admired the tiny pink creature sleeping so peacefully. 'She's so sweet. I've never actually seen a new baby before. Not in the flesh, I mean. I thought they were all red and wrinkled.'

'So was Emily at first. But she's just pink now. And very hungry. I've just fed her, which is why she's sleeping.' Cassie waved to the chair beside the bed. 'Come and sit down and let me thank you for holding the fort when I took off. Angus is very taken with you.'

'It's mutual! He woke up a couple of times, wanting Mummy, but between us Ben and I managed to settle him down.'

'Ah, yes—Ben. He seemed a bit disgruntled last night, not nearly as thrilled with you as his nephew. Told me you had a date and changed your mind about coming to see me.' Cassie's brown eyes gleamed. 'Is that right?'

'Certainly not!' said Kate hotly. 'I rang his office, but he was out and Dan Beaumont took a message for me. I'd forgotten my evening class, and much as I wanted to I couldn't skip it because I've got an exam looming.'

'Ah, I see.' Cassie smiled and handed Kate a card. 'This is Ben's home number. Give him a ring tonight and explain.'

Kate took the card and put it in her bag. No way was she going to ring Ben Fletcher and get a snub for her pains. She chatted for a while longer with Cassie, took a last look at the sleeping baby, then sighed. 'Time to go.' She looked up with a warm smile. 'I'm very relieved everything went well. We were pretty uptight by the time we heard the glad news.'

'So I gather. You did Ben a great service, keeping him occupied until Alec got back—not to mention coping with my son.' Cassie paused. 'You know, Kate, it's hard to remember I hadn't met you until recently. I feel I've known you for ever.'

Kate's eyes lit up. 'Really? I thought it was just me, being fanciful.'

'Not a bit of it. So please don't wait to be asked— call in and see us whenever you want. I'm going home tomorrow.'

'So soon? Shouldn't you stay longer?'

'No fear. Angus is missing me, and I hate being away from Alec. Besides, I'll be awash with helpers. My mother will be on hand for a day or so, as well as Caroline and Mrs Hicks—and probably Alec's invaluable Margaret too, after she's dealt with his patients.' Cassie laughed. 'It's a good thing I'm feeding Emily myself, otherwise I'd never get a chance to cuddle her.'

Kate reluctantly took her leave, then ran most of the way back to Hardacres, wishing her careful budget would have stretched to another taxi. She was dishevelled and wet when she got to the shop, with only a few minutes' grace to tidy herself up and check all was running smoothly before the first publishers' rep arrived.

She was snatching a much needed cup of coffee later that afternoon when a grinning Harry interrupted her to announce that there was an impatient male in the shop, demanding her presence.

Ben! thought Kate, and deliberately loosened a few strands of hair, put some lipstick on and took her glasses off. But it was a very small male who came running towards her, Caroline in hot pursuit.

'Kate!' called Angus, brandishing the toy car she'd bought him. 'Mummy said to say thank you.'

'Why, Angus, how lovely to see you.' Kate gave him a quick hug, smiling at Caroline. 'You've obviously been visiting.'

'We've been to the hopsital,' said Angus, before Caroline could get a word in. 'I saw the baby. She's *small*!' He extended his hands a couple of inches to illustrate and Kate laughed.

'I've seen her too. She's cute. And she'll soon grow.'

'Angus thought she'd be the same size as him, ready to play,' explained Caroline, grinning.

Kate spent a few more minutes talking to the excited little boy, then Caroline bore him off, reminding him that Grandma was waiting at home, a thought that obviously consoled him for parting with Kate. She waved them off at the door, then returned to the fray to help a large influx of students with their search for textbooks.

She was last to leave the premises later that evening.
Having made sure all customers were out of the building,
she closed down the computer system, locked away the
cash in the safe in the office, then put on her raincoat
and locked up the shop. As she hurried away a figure
darted after her.

'Kate!'

She turned swiftly, then smiled politely to cover her
disappointment. 'Hello, Dan. Cold better?'

'Somewhat,' he said thickly. 'Will you risk my germs
if I give you a lift home?'

Kate nodded. Her feet were aching, as usual at this
time of night. 'Thank you. I will.'

Dan led her across the street to a Porsche parked under
the chestnut trees, and Kate sank into the passenger seat
with a sigh of relief, glad to get out of the pouring rain.

'Hard day?' asked Dan, making no move to start the
car.

'No more than usual.' She turned to look at him. 'By
the way, what exactly did you say to Ben Fletcher when
you gave him my message?'

He shrugged. 'Told him you couldn't make it because
you had something else on. I couldn't remember what
exactly. Why? Was it important?'

'No. Not really. Could we go now, please? I want to
get home.'

Dan gave her a sharp glance then started the car, and
a few minutes later they were outside Waverley Lodge.

'Are you coming in to see Mrs Beaumont?' asked Kate.

'In a minute.' Dan paused, clearing his throat and
fidgeting a little. 'Look, Kate, there's something I think
I ought to tell you. About Ben.'

Kate stiffened. 'Oh?'

'If you're in danger of succumbing to the famous Fletcher charm take my tip, Kate. Don't.' His voice sounded troubled enough to make her uneasy.

'I'm not. But even if I were, what's the problem?'

Dan looked down at his hands, as though searching for the right words. Kate was at screaming point by the time he finally spoke.

'Look, Kate, this is just between you and me. OK? Promise you'll never breathe a word.'

'Do get on with it, Dan—if you think it's any of my business. Which, frankly, I doubt. Has Ben embezzled the company funds or something?'

'Lord, no,' he said vehemently. 'Nothing like that. Ben's invaluable to the firm. That's the point, really. My father turns a blind eye to Ben's personal life because he's so brilliant at his job.'

Personal life, thought Kate. 'Go on,' she said quietly. 'Is he such a womaniser, then? Does he steal other men's wives?'

'No. Nothing like that. In fact the girls are just a front, Kate.' Dan drew in a deep breath. 'Ben prefers blokes.'

Kate sat very still. At last she turned stunned grey eyes on Dan. 'Are you *serious*?'

He nodded. 'Only for pity's sake don't let on. It's a pretty well-kept secret. From his family most of all.'

'So how do *you* know?'

'I frequent the same gym.' Dan cleared his throat. 'There's a guy there who's—well, let's just say he's a very close friend of Ben's. It's all very hush-hush, of course. And who would suspect a strapping chap like Ben? It's why he never has a steady girlfriend. Lots of casual dates for a smokescreen, but nothing permanent.

Besides, he likes women. Lots of blokes of his persuasion do, you know.'

'Yes, I do know,' said Kate, fumbling with the seatbelt. 'Goodnight. Thanks for bringing me home.'

'When can I see you again?' he said eagerly. 'Tomorrow night?'

'Sorry. Evening class.'

'*Again?* When, then?'

'I'm pretty busy studying at the moment. I'll ring you after my exams next week.'

'Not until then?' Dan sounded mutinous, like a little boy denied a treat.

Kate shook her head and got out into the rain. 'Aren't you coming in to see your grandmother?'

'Better not. I might give her this cold.'

'Goodnight, then.' Kate ran up the path with a sudden burst of speed, suddenly desperate to close the door on the world and shut herself in her flat. Mrs Beaumont, she knew, would be riveted in front of her favourite soap at this time. Desperate to avoid a chat, Kate went up to the flat, switched on the lights and stripped off her raincoat. Now, she thought grimly, she knew why messengers with bad news got executed for their pains. She could kill Dan with her bare hands for telling her about Ben.

Kate had taken a bath and made herself a sandwich and was settled down with a pile of revision before she'd calmed down. Now that it was no longer a possibility she realised that in her heart of hearts she'd hoped Ben was attracted to her. After the night they'd spent together, brought unexpectedly close by crisis, she'd felt that Ben liked her as much as she liked him. A wry smile curved her lips. Maybe he did. It wasn't impossible. He might even want her for a friend. Whereas, thought Kate bitterly, looking the truth straight in the eye, she'd wanted *him* for a lover. And she'd come to Pennington looking for an escape from emotional quicksands! What a joke.

Kate worked like a demon next day, driving her staff hard when several deliveries of books arrived all at once, instead of on separate days as she'd arranged.

Harry and Gail went off to early lunch looking worn out, leaving Clare to man the till while Kate got to grips with a promotional display.

'You all right?' said Clare quietly in a lull.

'Fine. I just wanted to get everything sorted as quickly as possible.'

'You don't look fine.'

Kate managed a smile. 'It's my exams.'

'You'll sail through them!'

'I hope so. I can't afford to waste money on a course by failing, that's for sure.' She stiffened suddenly, biting her lip, conscious of colour draining from her face as Ben Fletcher strolled into the shop. Gail came rushing in behind him, badly out of breath, her face bright with hope, but Ben didn't even notice her. He came straight to Kate, smiling the famous smile.

'How about some lunch? I'll treat you to a sandwich and a coffee, or a pie and a pint, whichever you like.'

Having opened her mouth to refuse, Kate was startled to hear herself accept rather casually, as though this were something they did every day. 'Why, thanks. A sandwich, then.'

Ben turned the smile on Clare and Gail alike, the latter muttering something inaudible in answer to his casual, friendly enquiry about her health.

'The coffee-shop, then?' asked Ben a few minutes later as they walked along the pavement.

Kate, catching sight of their reflection in a shop window, let out a giggle which owed more to tension than mirth. 'Yes, right.'

'What's so funny?'

'You and me,' she shouted up at him as a gust of wind tore at her hair, bringing glossy black strands down to whip across her forehead. 'We look ridiculous together.'

'*I* don't think so. Hell, it's going to pour again. Take my hand. We'll make a run for it.' Ben hauled her along the pavement, his long legs covering the ground so fast that Kate had to race to keep up with him. They arrived in the coffee-shop breathless and dishevelled, a condition which did little for Kate's appearance, while wet, wind-blown hair merely added to Ben's attraction. There's no justice, she thought acidly. The place was full when they arrived, but by the time Ben had taken Kate's raincoat a corner table had become free and Kate slid behind it quickly, taken aback when Ben settled himself on the banquette beside her rather than taking the chair opposite.

'You looked a bit startled when I came in the shop,' he remarked once their order was given. 'Headache?'

'No.' How could she tell him that seeing him in the flesh for the first time after Dan's revelation had been hard to take in her stride? 'We had a busy morning. Lots of deliveries.' She held out her hands ruefully, displaying two broken fingernails. 'Occupational hazard.'

Ben clasped both her hands in one of his, and to her great disquiet casually kept them there until their coffee and sandwiches arrived.

Flustered for a wide variety of reasons, Kate took refuge in her salad roll, only to find her mouth so dry that she had difficulty in swallowing the first mouthful.

'Cassie told me you went to evening class on Monday,' said Ben, encountering no such problems with the hero sandwich he was demolishing. 'Your message to Dan obviously lost something in the translation. He told me you were having dinner with him.'

Kate turned to look at him in astonishment. 'I don't know why! I promised to have dinner with him some time, it's true. But Monday I went to my evening class. And tonight I do the same. Exams next week.'

Ben met her look thoughtfully. 'I was up to my neck in work—it's possible I misheard Dan.'

I wish I had, thought Kate in sudden despair. It was so difficult to sit here with Ben, his very dimensions making it impossible not to sit in close, warm contact, and still believe what Dan had told her.

'This is my second visit here in two weeks,' remarked Ben with a sudden grin. 'My usual lunchtime haunts are more male-orientated.'

A remark which brought Kate back to earth with a sickening crash.

'You've gone pale again,' said Ben swiftly. 'Are you coming down with something?'

Nothing he could do anything about, she thought miserably. 'No. It's the heat in here after the weather outside.' She smiled brightly. 'How do you like your new niece?'

'Terrifyingly small, isn't she?' He grinned. 'I prefer them like Angus, to be honest. I don't fancy handling little Emily until she grows a bit. But she's a sweet little scrap. And Cass looks marvellous. She's going home today.'

'So I gather. I hope she doesn't overdo things.'

Ben scrutinised her closely. 'You really like my sister, don't you?'

'Very much.'

'Do you like me too?' he asked baldly, and his eyes, so unexpectedly dark beneath the bright hair, turned to lock with hers in a way which made it impossible to lie.

'Yes,' said Kate, equally baldly.

'Even though we got off to such a bad start?'

More of a bad start than you know, thought Kate despondently. 'I soon found out the truth.'

'Then does that mean we can be friends?'

Kate looked at him for a long moment. 'You want that?'

'I wouldn't have thought so before the other night, I'll admit. But those hours we spent together revealed a lot—to both of us. And what I learned about you I like very much.' He looked down into his coffee-cup, his face oddly stern. 'This is going to sound like the worst kind of conceit, but because of the way I look most women want to make love rather than conversation. To find a woman I can talk to—other than Cass—is something of a discovery.'

Kate stared unseeingly across the crowded restaurant. Everything Ben was saying underlined what Dan had told her. If Ben wanted to be friends, and meant them to spend some time together, could she cope, in the circumstances?

'You're very quiet,' he said after a while. 'Look, if you'd rather I got lost just say so.'

'No!' said Kate involuntarily. And the very fact that her reaction had been so swift told her how badly she wanted any kind of relationship he had to offer. On any terms. She smiled. 'All right. Friends it is.'

Ben patted the hands she hadn't even been conscious she'd been clenching in her lap. 'Thank you, Kate.' He smiled wryly. 'Cass obviously wants you to be a regular visitor at the Neville residence. It makes it easier all round if you and I are on a friendly footing.'

Not easier all round exactly, thought Kate as Ben left her at the bookshop. For everyone else, including Ben, maybe. But for herself it was going to take some getting used to. Ben Fletcher was the best-looking man she'd laid eyes on in her entire life, and one look at him was enough to send the blood leaping through her veins in the kind of response it had never made to a man before. Until now she hadn't dared to admit it, even to herself. But now, when it was never to be put to the test, she knew that her resistance would have been short-lived if Ben had ever asked more of her than friendship.

CHAPTER SIX

IN SPITE of teasing from Clare and veiled reproach from
Gail, Kate began to enjoy life enormously after the lunch
with Ben. He took her out to dinner on Saturday night
and came in the Range Rover to take her to the Nevilles'
for coffee and baby worship the following morning, afterwards driving her to lunch at a pub several country
miles from Pennington.

They drove through Cotswold hills bright with cool
March sunshine, past fields dotted white with lambs and
cottage gardens bright with daffodils. Conversation never
flagged. They found common ground on a variety of
subjects from literature and the latest technology in
computers to the prospects of the England cricket team
in the forthcoming season.

'For a girl with no brothers you know a lot about
sport,' commented Ben over lunch.

'Dad's a fanatic. And when I was a student I knew a
lot of sporting types. Rowdy lot, most of them. One of
my boyfriends rowed for his college.' She drank some
of her cider shandy. 'What about you?'

'I played lock forward for the first fifteen at rugby,
hence the dent in the nose, and bowled medium fast for
the first eleven at cricket.' Ben grinned. 'My height came
in handy.'

'I'll bet it did.'

'What did you play?'

86

'Tennis—badly, though I swim quite well. But my favourite pastime is reading.'

'Just as well with your job!'

'Why do you think I chose it?' She pulled a face. 'It certainly isn't for the money.'

'Ever fancied writing, like Cass?'

'Oh, yes. Once I finish cramming for my business qualification I might even have a shot at it.'

'What genre? Crime?'

'More a study in human relationships,' said Kate casually. 'One should always write about things familiar, they say. I could write about my experiences with Ally and the others in London. Take each girl as a character and weave a story about her which interlocks with the others. It's a popular concept.'

'And would your personal story have a happy ending?' said Ben softly.

Kate's face shadowed. 'I could always make one up.'

When they returned to Pennington Kate was glad of her particular domestic arrangements at Waverley Lodge. There was no question of asking a man in for coffee, even under very different circumstances, when another escort might expect to round off the day by taking her to bed.

'Thank you for a lovely day,' said Kate as the Range Rover stopped outside the Lodge. 'It was a treat to get out into the country.'

'What will you do this evening?'

'Cram any knowledge I possibly can into this brain of mine, ready for the exam tomorrow.'

Ben smiled, leaned across and kissed her cheek. 'Good luck, Kate; don't stay up too late.'

'I won't. Goodnight.'

When Kate got in Mrs Beaumont emerged from her sitting room.

'Pleasant day, dear?'

'Very. Lunch in a country pub—quite a treat.'

'Young Dan was here earlier. He asked if you'd give him a ring when you got back.'

Kate took the slip of paper with Dan's number on it, promised to ring when she got up to the flat and bade Mrs Beaumont goodnight.

'Kate?' said Dan when she rang him. 'I called round to see you but Gran said you were out for the day.'

'I've just got back.'

'Where did you go?'

'I had lunch in the country.'

'Who with?'

'Dan, I don't think that's any of your business,' said Kate gently.

'Oops! Sorry. I just wanted to wish you good luck with your exams.'

'Thank you.'

'When do you finish?'

'Wednesday.'

'Then how about dinner on Thursday?'

Kate paused, not very keen to accept, but she did so in the end. There was no reason at all why she shouldn't, she told herself, certainly not just because Ben Fletcher wanted her for a friend.

When Kate emerged, shattered, from the college at nine-thirty the following Wednesday night, she was surprised—and deeply delighted—to find Ben leaning against his Range Rover among the cars parked outside in the road.

'Ben! This is a nice surprise.'

'I hoped it would be.' He caught her hand in his. 'Well? How did it go?'

She shrugged, laughing. 'Haven't a clue. I'm numb. I finished the papers and that's about all I can remember.'

'Are you hungry?'

'Starving,' said Kate in surprise. Food had not been high on her agenda since lunch with Ben the previous Sunday.

'I've got a hamper in the car. I thought we could go back to my place and picnic.' He opened the car door and lifted her up into the passenger seat. 'Approved?'

'Why, yes, it's a lovely idea. Where do you live?'

'Not far from Cassie and Alec—the garden flat in one of those big old houses overlooking the park.' Ben nosed the car out into the road and the stream of traffic leaving the college. 'Before that I had a very modern place, all chrome and black and white. My minimalist period,' he said with a grin. 'Now I'm into club chairs and chesterfield sofas. It suits Griff and me very well.'

Griff, thought Kate with sudden dread. 'I—I won't be able to stay long,' she said breathlessly. 'I had my day off on Monday to swot. I wish now I'd arranged for it for tomorrow.'

'You'll be home before midnight, I promise, Cinderella,' he said indulgently. 'And Cassie and Mrs Hicks filled the hamper, so supper will be forthcoming the moment we get in.'

When Ben turned into the drive of one of the big old Edwardian houses on Burford Crescent Kate looked rather wistfully at the lighted, welcoming windows of the ground-floor flat. This could all have been so different, she thought, if only Ben...

She gave him a bright smile to disguise her sudden melancholy as he lifted her down.

'Come on,' he said, reaching for the hamper. 'I'll introduce you to Griff.'

Kate followed the tall, athletic figure up the steps to the front door, tense with apprehension as Ben unlocked it and ushered her into a high, lofty hall. There was a thumping noise from behind the door at the end, and she looked up at Ben questioningly. He grinned and went to open the door, letting out a golden retriever ecstatic with delight at the sight of his master.

'Griff!' said Ben warningly, and at once the dog was quiet, wagging his tail in pleasure, his manners perfect as Ben introduced him to Kate.

Her relief was so violent that she fell to her knees and put her arms round the dog's neck, receiving wet, enthusiastic kisses in response. 'How lovely to meet you, Griff,' she assured the animal huskily.

'You obviously like dogs!' Ben helped her up. 'Come on. I waited to eat with you. I'm hungry.'

The functional kitchen had pine cupboards, white working surfaces, and surprisingly little clutter for a man who lived alone. Ben set a large tray with cutlery and glasses while Kate took the food from the hamper. Cassie had provided thick slices of ham, a bowl of green salad, ready tossed, part of a raised game pie, crusty brown rolls and a foil package which yielded thin wafers of smoked salmon. Ben filled two dinner plates with a selection of food and put them on the tray.

'If you look in the fridge you'll find a bottle of champagne,' he said casually. 'Bring it through, but leave Griff in the kitchen. He's had his supper.'

Kate apologised to the mournful dog as she shut the kitchen door on him, then followed Ben into a high-ceilinged room with what looked like several miles of heavy, padded curtain looped back at either side of the wide window embrasure. Ben put down the tray on a low round table in the middle of the room, then drew the curtains and waved Kate to one of the large leather chairs placed at either side of the fireplace. He shook out a napkin with a flourish, handed it to Kate with a knife and fork, gave her one of the plates of food, then removed the cork from the champagne bottle with only a hiss of smoke to mark its passing. He filled a pair of crystal flutes, gave one to Kate, collected his own share of the food and settled his large frame on the suitably roomy chesterfield couch which dominated the room.

Ben raised his glass to Kate. 'To success in your exams, Kate.'

'Amen to that,' she said with feeling, and drank some champagne before making a start on the simple, deeply satisfying meal. 'What a treat this is!'

'Cass's choice—she usually has smoked salmon for a celebration.'

'We had sandwiches of it the day Cassie took me to lunch,' said Kate indistinctly.

'She looked on it as a special occasion, then.'

'It was to me,' said Kate sincerely, and looked across at him, thinking he had no right to look so devastating. It just wasn't fair. The muted light from the gold-shaded lamps turned his hair to silver gilt. Tonight he wore a heavy oatmeal wool sweater over a white shirt, his long legs encased in pale cords old enough to fit him like a glove. Kate, in her pink jersey and faded jeans, her hair pulled back in a braid, felt the contrast keenly.

Ben got up to refill both their glasses. 'Don't worry,' he said, smiling into her questioning eyes. 'I've ordered a taxi for later so I can join in the celebration. If I drove you home I'd have to abstain.'

'You're very thoughtful,' said Kate rather unsteadily, and drank half the champagne down before going on with her meal.

'What else are friends for?' said Ben. 'Cassie sent her love, by the way.'

Kate accepted the change of subject with relief, happy to discuss Angus and the new baby, and anything in the Neville household that Ben cared to mention. Restricting the conversation to the interesting but everyday journals of the Fletcher/Neville households was like learning to ride a bicycle, she thought ruefully. She needed to keep going in case she fell off into the dark waters of her personal response to a man who would never reciprocate in kind.

But when Ben went off to the kitchen to fetch cheese and fruit Kate pulled herself together firmly. Ben Fletcher was such an overpoweringly handsome man, it was unlikely he'd have wanted an ordinary girl like Kate Harker for a lover even if his tastes had been different. He wants you for a friend, she reminded herself stringently. And why? Precisely because you're not one of the pretty, slender types who expect a love affair. You're safe. Someone comfortable he can talk to and take out without any danger of complications. And at the same time provide a cover for the other side of his life.

'That's a very pensive look,' said Ben, returning. 'Penny for your thoughts.'

'Too expensive by far,' she said lightly, and helped herself to an apple.

'No cheese?'

'Not at this time of night. I'll never sleep.'

Ben looked at her for a moment. 'There are remedies for insomnia, Kate.'

She munched on her apple doggedly, ignoring the nuance of suggestion in his tone. 'Normally I never need any. I'm so tired after a day on my feet followed by a session of feverish swotting, I sleep the moment my head touches the pillow.'

He grinned. 'I meant a session or two at the gym— nothing untoward!'

Kate laughed. 'I'm not very energetic, I'm afraid. Pumping iron isn't my idea of fun.'

'Weights aren't the only thing on offer at my club. How about aerobics, or badminton, squash—even table tennis?'

She shook her head. 'No, thanks. I get enough exercise at the store, carrying boxes round.' Ben's club, she felt, was a place to avoid like the plague.

Ben looked at her, eyes narrowed, for a moment, then changed the subject. 'By the way, I'm bidden to tell you that Pennington General holds a hospital ball every year. End of April and fancy dress as usual, heaven help us. Alec asked if you'd like to join the Neville party. Cassie should be able to leave the baby for a few hours by then. Will you come as my partner?'

This was so *hard*, thought Kate despairingly. Ben Fletcher was doing—and asking—all the right things, and all of it for the wrong reasons. Not that it made any difference. If Ben wanted to take her to a ball wild horses wouldn't keep her away.

'I'd love to,' she said with perfect truth. 'But fancy dress?'

'Afraid so.'

'I'll have to think about it.' She grinned. 'How about you? You're the fitness fanatic—go as Mr Universe.'

'No chance,' he said, pulling a face. 'Anyway, they've got a theme. Opera, would you believe?'

'Spoilt for choice, then,' said Kate promptly. 'Samson, Radames from *Aïda*—plenty of chances to bare your chest.'

'No way am I baring my chest,' he retorted. 'Not at a charity ball, anyway.' He leered at her theatrically. 'In private, with an audience of one, it's a different thing— Hey! What's the matter? What have I said? I was only joking, Kate.'

'I know. Indigestion,' she lied, trying to banish vivid, unbearable pictures from her mind. She got up abruptly. 'It must be about time for my taxi.'

'Not yet.' He covered the space between them and took hold of her hands, looking down into her face. 'Kate, look at me.'

Reluctantly she lifted her eyes to his.

'I said friends, remember?' he reminded her, frowning. 'You looked as if I was about to leap on you and demand your body in return for your supper.'

'You're utterly wrong,' she said with bleak honesty. 'I never thought that for a moment.'

'Then what is it?' he persisted, baffled.

'I'm just tired.' She forced a smile. 'It's been a long day.'

Ben looked at her for a moment longer, then very gently he drew her against him until she was leaning against his chest. He held her loosely with one arm, his other hand smoothing her hair as though she were a child in need of comfort. 'You need what Angus calls a snuggle,' he said huskily.

Kate allowed herself the luxury of the contact for a moment or two, but proximity to Ben Fletcher's superbly fit body so quickly became a torment that she moved away, her colour high.

'What I really need,' she said brightly, 'is a cup of tea if there's time. And if you have any, of course.'

'There is and I do,' he replied, with a crooked smile. 'Come and talk to Griff while I make it.'

Kate went with him to the kitchen, insisting that she wash dishes while Ben made tea for her.

'I'll finish off the champagne,' he said as he handed her a mug. 'I wish I knew what was going on behind those big grey eyes of yours, Kate Harker. You shy away like a startled little pony if I get too close. Did one of those London blokes of yours get too rough with you some time? Or is it just a physical aversion to my person?' he added, not quite casually enough.

Kate shook her head. 'No to both.' She bent to pat the dog's smooth, toffee-coloured head, then went through the door Ben held open for her. 'You were imagining things.'

'If you say so.' Ben took her hand. 'To prove it come and sit beside me on this smart new sofa of mine while we wait for your taxi.'

Kate sat, clutching her mug of tea like a shield, then suddenly her sense of humour reasserted itself and she gave a little chuckle.

'That's better,' said Ben. 'But why the laugh?'

'I was laughing at myself, for being such a goose.'

'You mean you've finally decided I'm not going to cross this line you've marked out between us!'

She turned to look him in the eye. 'Actually I never thought you would.' Which was true enough. It was her own reactions which frightened her, not Ben's.

'Good.' His eyes moved over her consideringly. 'Cassie, by the way, fancies herself as Tosca for the costume ball. Something to do with her waistline. Who do you go for?'

Kate grinned. 'Well, we can rule out *La Traviata* and *La Bohème*, for a start, because Violetta and Mimi were both wasting away with consumption. I'm a bit robust for either lady. I'll give it some thought. How about you?'

'Something inconspicuous!'

Privately doubting that Ben would look inconspicuous whatever he wore, Kate finished her tea and set the mug down on the table beside her. 'It was very good of you to lay all this on for me tonight, Ben,' she said, turning to him.

'I merely had the idea of helping you celebrate. Cassie saw to the food.'

'My thanks to you both, then. I'll ring Cassie to thank her tomorrow—'

'But I'm here tonight,' he pointed out softly. 'You can thank me right now. Like this.' And, taking both her hands in his, Ben bent his bright head and kissed her mouth gently, then drew in a sharp breath and kissed her again, anything but gently. This wasn't fair, she thought frenziedly; then the doorbell rang and they jumped apart.

'My taxi,' gasped Kate.

'Saved by the bell,' said Ben drily, and helped her on with her raincoat. 'Don't look like that, Kate. It was only a kiss between two consenting adults.' He seized her by the elbows as the colour drained from her face. 'What is it? Are you ill?'

'No. Just a bit tired suddenly.' Kate managed a smile. 'Thank you again. It was a very nice surprise.'

Her last sight of Ben with the hall light behind him was as a tall, dark silhouette with a halo of gold for hair. He looked unreal, which was a good way for her to think of him. If he hadn't mentioned consenting adults after that earth-shattering kiss, Kate thought miserably as the taxi bore her home, she could have had daydreams about being the woman to change his life. But dreams they were. And the sooner she came to terms with the hard facts of life the better.

CHAPTER SEVEN

CLARE was deeply impressed by Kate's invitation to the costume ball. 'Robert says it's the event of the season in little old Pennington. What will you wear?'

'That's the snag,' said Kate ruefully. 'It's an operatic theme, worse luck. Is there a place here where I can hire something for peanuts? My cash-flow's dried to a trickle until pay day.'

Clare waved an imaginary wand. 'Don't worry—meet your fairy godmother. I'm a whizz with a sewing machine.'

Kate made a token protest about taking up Clare's time, but this was brushed aside.

'My darling's away at least three days a week, as you well know. I'd be glad of something to do. Which heroine do you fancy?'

Kate pulled a face. 'None of them much—so many of them are frail and ailing. Not exactly me, is it?'

'True—but I bet you could roll a mean cigar on your thigh!'

'Carmen?' Kate drank down her coffee, eyes brightening. 'Not bad. I'm the right sort of colouring—'

'Get that hair curled and teased out a bit, slap a flower behind your ear and I'll run up a frilly little number with cheap lining material. We'll go shopping tomorrow lunchtime.' Clare chuckled. 'Mind you, there'll probably be dozens of Carmens.'

'Perfect. I crave anonymity.'

Clare pointed out that with Ben Fletcher as a partner this was unlikely whatever Kate wore. 'What's his choice?'

'No idea, except that he refuses to bare his chest.'

'What a spoilsport!'

Kate jumped to her feet, yawning. 'Time to return to the fray. Lord, I'm tired. I wish I hadn't said I'd go out tonight.'

Clare's eyebrows shot into her hair. 'Ben *again*?'

'No. Dan Beaumont. I've already put him off once, so I couldn't bring myself to do it again.' Kate smiled gratefully. 'Thanks for the Carmen idea, Clare. I owe you.'

'I'll enjoy it. And now your exams are over you can do the rough sewing.'

Kate chuckled. 'It's the only kind I know!'

Dan Beaumont came for Kate promptly at eight that evening, spent a few minutes with his grandmother, then bore Kate off to the restaurant currently most patronised by the young and prosperous of Pennington Spa. It was the type of place Kate's wardrobe failed to cater for. She had very little money to spare for what she thought of as party gear. In London it had been easier, since all four flatmates had constantly borrowed from each other. Now, with only her own wardrobe to rely on, Kate wore a plain black shift dress bought at a bargain price in a sale, added a long string of *faux* pearls and wore more make-up than usual. The effect, it seemed, was satisfactory. Dan was extravagant with his compliments.

The restaurant was crowded and noisy, and Dan seemed to know everyone there, making a great show of waving and smiling as he led Kate to their table. His expensive Italian-designed suit was pearl-grey, his tie was hand-painted silk to match the handkerchief thrust into a breast pocket, and the moment the waiter arrived Dan ordered Bellinis without consulting Kate, which got things off on the wrong foot. The evening went rapidly downhill. Dan seemed to think he was impressing her by sending away the claret he'd chosen, complaining about his steak, treating the waiters like dirt, in between times regaling her with his genius at Beaumont Electronics, and all the time looking round to see if they were being noticed.

Kate was heartily glad when it was time to leave, but when Dan drove off, still extolling the brilliance of his plans for his father's company, she had to interrupt him to point out that he was driving in the wrong direction.

'I thought we'd have a coffee at my place before I get you back. You can't ask me up to your flat at Waverley Lodge,' he said, winking.

'Drive me there right now, nevertheless,' ordered Kate angrily. 'I said yes to dinner, Dan, nothing else.'

He promptly parked the car and reached for her. The ensuing exchange was short and anything but sweet, brought to an end by Kate punching Dan viciously on the nose. He howled in rage, then drove a furious, dishevelled Kate back to Waverley Lodge, where she re-iterated icy thanks for her dinner as she jumped out of the car. Dan, equally furious, barely gave her time to stand clear before he gunned the Porsche away down the quiet street.

Friday, as usual, was hectic. A half-hour spent with Clare shopping for her Carmen finery was the only break in

the day. It was after seven when Kate locked up the shop,
hefted the parcel of material and turned to find Ben
smiling down at her.

'I come seeking a favour,' he said, taking the parcel
from her. 'I hope you're free tonight. If I drive you home
will you join me in a spot of baby-sitting for Cass?'

Kate, weary to the bone a moment before, suddenly
felt on top of the world. 'Of course I will.'

Ben ushered her into the Range Rover waiting illegally
at the kerb. 'Sorry it's such short notice. I rang you last
night but no luck, then again at lunchtime but Gail said
you were out. Did she give you the message?'

'She must have forgotten.'

'Or something.' Ben's lips tightened. 'Anyway, where
were you when I rang?'

'Shopping for cheap shiny satin,' she said demurely.

He laughed. 'For *you*?'

'No, for Carmen. Clare suggested it for the ball.'

'Clever girl, Clare,' he said brusquely.

'Come in and talk to Mrs Beaumont while I change,'
coaxed Kate. 'She loves visitors. You can ring Cassie
and tell her I'm coming. I'll only be ten minutes or so.'

Mrs Beaumont was only too pleased to entertain the
young man her son thought so highly of while Kate
rushed through a shower, took down her hair, searched
feverishly through her wardrobe for something suitable,
and eventually ran downstairs with her raincoat over her
arm, wearing jeans, her silk shirt and a long black car-
digan from the men's department of her favourite chain
store.

'Ten and a half minutes,' said Ben, amazed, checking
his watch, and winked at Mrs Beaumont. 'A pearl among
women!'

'I hurried because Cassie's going out,' Kate said, pulling a face at him.

'Damn!' he said, grinning. 'And there was I, Mrs B, thinking she was rushing for my sake.'

'You take care of her, Benedict Fletcher,' said the old lady, smiling. 'No keeping her out till all hours.'

He bent to kiss the small, arthritic hand. 'She'll be safe with me, I promise.'

More's the pity, thought Kate sadly as they drove off to the Neville house.

'Where's Cassie going?' she asked.

'Out for a meal. Alec wants his wife to himself for an hour or two between the baby's feeds, and because Caroline's off sick with flu I volunteered our services.' Ben stopped the car outside the tall house and came round to lift Kate down. He held her by the elbows for a moment once she was on her feet. 'Did I take you too much for granted?'

'No, of course not. I'm happy to help Cassie.'

'Which I told her. So try and persuade her it's a good idea to go out tonight.'

Alec Neville threw open the door before they could ring, a broad smile on his face. 'Hello, Kate. This is very good of you.'

Kate assured him that it was no hardship at all. Her baby-sitting services were available any time she was free. 'No experience, but I learn fast.'

They went upstairs to find Cassie reading to her small son in the sitting room. She looked up as she caught sight of Kate, laughing as Angus abandoned his mother shamelessly now that the new playmates had arrived.

'Are you sure you want to do this, Kate?' Cassie asked, getting up.

'Turn down an evening with Angus and me?' said Ben. 'No chance.'

Cassie held out her hand to Kate. 'Come and see Emily, then I'll just do something to my face and I'm ready.'

'I booked dinner for eight, darling,' said Alec. 'So get a move on. I'm sure Kate and Ben can cope for an hour or two.'

'I know, I know,' said Cassie, pulling a face. 'I wouldn't go out otherwise, and in any case Ben's got the number of the restaurant.'

Upstairs, in a Moses basket alongside her parents' bed, Emily Catherine Neville lay sleeping, half turned on her side.

'I've just fed her,' said Cassie softly, 'so with luck she'll sleep until I get back.' She showed Kate where all the baby's equipment was kept, including the all-important baby-listener, then they both went on tiptoe from the room.

'I'll finish getting ready in the bathroom,' said Cassie on the landing, then smiled. 'I hope all this doesn't put you off babies for life.'

Since Kate, for one reason and another, couldn't envisage babies being part of her life at all for the foreseeable future, she shook her head, smiling. 'I'm madly in love with Angus, for starters. And although I'm a bit nervous about Emily I'll do my best. And Ben's on hand for support.'

Alec Neville finally bore off his wife, cutting short her instructions and last-minute qualms as he hurried her down to the car.

Ben returned to the sitting room, grinning. 'Alec's finally managed to get Cass through the door, but how long he'll be able to keep her out is another thing. She reminded me that—'

'Boiled water's in the fridge, bottle-warmer's on the counter, there's a casserole sitting on the Aga for us and Angus goes to bed in half an hour,' recited Kate, chuckling.

'Full marks.' Ben sat down beside her with a sigh, taking Angus onto his lap. 'Right, then, Scheherazade, tell us a story.'

'Her name's Kate,' said Angus, puzzled.

'I know, sport. The other name's a sort of pet name— a joke between Kate and me.'

'I prefer Kate,' stated the little boy firmly, then leaned back against his uncle's broad chest to listen.

At first it was very hard for Kate to read the story and listen for Emily at the same time, but she quickly grew used to the odd little baby snufflings coming over the intercom. She finished the story for Angus, read him another, then accompanied him upstairs to his room with Ben. While Ben was tucking his nephew into bed Kate went into the main bedroom, hung over the cot for a while, gazing down at the sleeping baby, then went back to kiss Angus goodnight.

'Now,' said Ben, once they were back downstairs, 'we shall take the baby-listener to the kitchen and consume the supper Mrs Hicks has left for us as quickly as we can while we've got some peace. Angus will come down if he needs anything, because he just told me his sister can be very noisy. He's as keen to avoid waking her as we are.'

'Good lad!' Kate laughed as she stirred the creamy beef casserole on the Aga. 'Cassie said there's some rice in the warming oven and some ready-dressed salad greens in the fridge.'

'Coming up.' Ben put the salad on the table, then began slicing a crusty baton of bread. 'I'm starving.'

Kate set a generous serving of rice and beef in horse-radish sauce in front of him, then put her ear to the baby-listener.

'Relax.' Ben smiled at her lazily, and Kate turned away to serve herself, wondering if he felt the intimacy of the situation as much as she did. Probably not, which was a shame.

'Mm, this is delicious!' she said after the first mouthful.

'Better than the dinner you had last night?'

She looked up at him sharply. 'You heard about that?'

'Oh, yes. Dan was at great pains to tell me about his fabulous evening with you.' Ben helped himself to more salad. 'Like some of this?'

'Yes, please.' Kate ate in silence for a moment, then eyed him wryly. 'Actually the evening wasn't fabulous at all. Dan seemed to think he had to impress me with Bellinis and the most expensive dishes on the menu— without consulting me!' she added, eyes kindling.

'Where did he take you?'

'The Brasserie—the new place in Sussex Gardens.'

Ben nodded, unsurprised. 'The latest craze with Dan's set. I hear the food's good.'

'It ought to be. It costs a fortune.'

The meal over, Kate pushed her plate away with a sigh. 'But it wasn't a patch on this casserole Mrs Hicks did for us—which I enjoyed far more.'

'Maybe it's the company.' Ben leaned back in his chair, looking at her. 'I'm conceited enough to hope you might prefer an evening with me to one with Dan. Put me right if I'm wrong.'

'You're not,' she said candidly, meeting his eyes. 'Maybe you won't take this as a compliment, but I feel comfortable with you. Last night I felt very uncomfortable with Dan. He seemed to be putting on a show for me. Lord knows why.'

'I'm told it's his usual opening gambit.' Ben got up and fetched a platter of cheeses. 'Like some?'

Kate shook her head. 'No, thanks. I think I'd better go up and look at the baby.'

Ben frowned. 'Maybe it wasn't a good idea to saddle you with this tonight after a hard day's work.'

'Nonsense.' Kate got up, smiling sweetly. 'You can clear away and load the dishwasher while I do the baby check. Or does that offend your masculinity?' She stopped, blushing to the roots of her hair.

Ben stared in astonishment. 'It doesn't, I assure you.'

Kate murmured something incoherent and fled, glad to retreat upstairs to Emily, who was showing ominous signs of stirring. Small hands flailed, the downy head turned from one side to another and suddenly the rosepetal mouth opened and Emily let out a wail.

Kate picked her up gingerly, supporting the downy head with one hand as she cuddled the baby against her shoulder. But Emily went on wailing. And Kate, with a sinking heart, soon discovered why. Miss Neville was in crying need of a fresh nappy.

'What's up?' asked Ben softly, coming into the room.

'Nappy-change!' said Kate tersely, and carefully transferred his niece to his reluctant embrace. 'Just hang onto her for a minute while I get her gear together, then I'll have a shot at it.'

She laid the changing mat on the floor, assembled a fresh disposable nappy and the various baby-wipes and creams Cassie had shown her, then took the still wailing baby from her large uncle's panicking grasp. Kate laid the baby on the mat, undid the poppers on the tiny sleeping suit and exposed Emily's lower half with un-skilled hands. It took several minutes and a couple of discarded nappies before the baby was clean and dry and securely fastened up again, by which time Emily was wide awake and vociferous and her attendants were in a state of mental exhaustion.

'Why's she crying?' demanded Angus sleepily, wan-dering into the room.

Ben picked him up, rubbing his cheek against the curly hair. 'Kate had to change her nappy.'

'And I've never done it before,' Kate told him rue-fully as she wrapped a cot blanket round the baby. 'I'm going to take her downstairs and give her some water. Would you like some juice, Angus?'

The little boy nodded sleepily.

When Cassie and Alec returned home, they found their daughter fast asleep on Kate's shoulder in the sitting room, a Schubert quintet playing very softly on the stereo, and Ben stretched out in the armchair sleeping as soundly as his niece.

There was much muted laughter as Ben came awake in a hurry, full of apologies as he jumped to his feet. Cassie hurried to relieve Kate of her daughter, but Kate smiled cajolingly.

'Couldn't I hold her a little longer? It took some doing to get her to sleep after we changed her nappy, but I've enjoyed cuddling her this past half-hour.'

'Half an hour!' said Alec, amused. 'And have you been out for the count all that time, Ben?'

'Most of it,' Ben admitted guiltily, smiling wryly at Kate. 'I helped—a bit—with the nappy-change. Moral support more than anything. Then we thought a spot of soothing music might help get Emily back to sleep—and that's the last I remember.'

Cassie chuckled. 'Give me five minutes to change out of my glad rags then I'll make some coffee. Sure you're OK, Kate?'

Kate was only too happy to go on cuddling the sleeping baby. This, she thought, looking down at the little face at her breast, was the easy, enjoyable part.

'You look very comfortable,' commented Ben, when the Nevilles had gone to see their son. 'As though you've handled babies all your life.'

'At the moment it's easy. This part I love. The nappy-change was terrifying.'

'For you and me both!' he said with feeling, then fell silent, watching her. 'Thanks, Kate. No one else I know would give up a Friday night to do this.'

'What else are friends for?' she said lightly, looking up. 'I had nothing better to do.'

'I thought you might be going out with Dan again,' he said casually.

'I won't be doing that again. Nor,' she added, with a crooked smile, 'will Dan ask me, I fancy.'

'Why not?'

Kate pulled a face. 'Let's say the evening rather fell short of his expectations.'

A smile lit Ben's eyes. 'Ah! Bit of a let-down after Dan's expenditure for the evening. He usually gets better results for the initial outlay. It's a well-known boast of his.'

Kate wrinkled her nose in disgust. 'You mean he discusses his social life at work?'

'With those who'll listen, yes.'

'Ugh!'

'I don't. Listen, I mean.'

'Good— Shh! I think she's about to wake.' Kate smiled tenderly down at the baby, then up at Ben, surprising a very thoughtful expression on his face. Then Cassie and Alec returned, the latter bearing a coffee-tray, and Emily Neville was handed over to her mother, leaving Kate with an odd sense of loss.

Cassie went upstairs to feed her daughter, leaving Alec to tease his baby-sitters about their exhausting evening.

'I'd like to have been there when you were helping with the nappy-change, Ben,' he laughed. 'Preferably with a camera.'

'Laugh all you like,' said Ben with dignity, 'I was rigid with fear that I'd drop the little scrap. Anyway, Kate did all the dirty work. *And* got Emily back to sleep. I'm impressed. I thought my niece wouldn't stop protesting until Cassie got back with her supper.'

Kate, more tired than she'd have believed possible, sat in a pleasant daze while Alec handed round coffee and offered port and brandy, which neither of his guests accepted, due to their advanced state of exhaustion.

'To think Cass copes with episodes like that as a matter of course,' said Ben in awe, 'and looks after Angus most of the time, writes best-sellers—'

'And happens to be the best wife a man could wish for, too,' said Alec, with such sincerity that Kate felt a lump in her throat, wondering if she'd ever inspire such deep feeling in a man.

When Cassie came back she found the trio discussing costumes for the hospital ball, and exclaimed with pleasure when she heard that Kate was coming as Carmen. 'Perfect, Kate. I've plumped for Tosca—and I do mean plumped! I'm hoping one of those high-waisted frocks will flatter my post-Emily waistline. And Alec can come as Cavaradossi, her artist lover, in a painter's smock and a floppy bow-tie.' She fixed her brother with a steely eye. 'So what about you, Benedict Fletcher? Any ideas yet?'

'No,' he said gloomily. 'I certainly can't match up with Kate.'

Kate giggled. 'True. You're more Viking than Latin. How about something Wagnerian? Siegfried—'

'I vote for a complete disguise as Othello,' said Alec, laughing. 'A bit of boot polish and a wig—'

'That's a thought,' said Ben, brightening, and Cassie hooted.

'You've got to be joking!'

'I may surprise you all,' he said, looking smug. 'In fact an idea has just occurred to me. I shall keep it secret and burst in on you in all my glory on the night.'

'Does everyone go in fancy dress to these things?' asked Kate a short time later as Ben drove her home.

'You bet. Some of the consultants' wives compete with each other ferociously, even hire stuff from London.'

'Golly,' said Kate, thinking of her bargain-tray satin. 'I hope I don't let the side down.'

'You'll make a fantastic Carmen,' he assured her, stopping outside Waverley Lodge. 'Though not the only one, probably.'

'I'm counting on it,' she assured him. 'I jumped at the idea so I wouldn't stand out in the crowd.'

'Why?' he asked curiously.

'Not my scene. I was never any good at drama. My school prided itself on the plays it put on, but the only thing I did on stage was change the scenery!'

Ben laughed. 'Actually I may grumble but these costume affairs are great fun. You'll enjoy it.'

'I'm sure I will.' Kate smiled at him, then yawned suddenly. 'Gosh, I'm tired.'

'You were magnificent. Thank you, Kate. Cassie would never have gone out if you hadn't volunteered.'

'I was press-ganged! Not that I minded,' Kate added hurriedly. 'In fact I now feel qualified to cope any time Cassie wants a break. Could you mention it when you talk to her next?'

'Ring her up and tell her yourself.'

'Right, I will.'

'What are you doing tomorrow night?' he asked.

'Nothing much,' she said warily.

'There's a Tom Stoppard play on at the theatre. If I can get tickets would you like to go?' Ben bent his head to peer into her face.

'You don't have to—I mean, just because I helped out tonight you don't have to make it up to me,' she muttered.

Ben reached out a hand and turned her face up to his. 'What a lot of nonsense you talk, Miss Harker. I'm asking you to the theatre because it's a good play and I'd like your company. Do you want to come or not?'

'Yes,' said Kate, and he kissed her square on her surprised mouth.

'Good. What time to do you finish on Saturdays?'

'Six,' she managed.

'I'll pick you up just before seven and feed you after the show.' Ben laid a finger on her lower lip, smiled at her, then leaned across to undo her seatbelt.

Kate shrank back into her seat, away from the warmth and scent of his body, afraid he'd realise how his nearness affected her.

'Stop it,' he said sternly, sitting upright. 'I'm not Dan Beaumont, Kate. You're in no danger from me, I promise.'

That's the trouble, she thought ruefully as she ran up the path to the house. I wish I were.

CHAPTER EIGHT

KATE eventually achieved hard-won acceptance where Ben Fletcher was concerned. There were no hard and fast rules in her relationship with him, but soon it was taken for granted that they spent one evening in the week together, and most Saturdays other than the times she went home to Guildford to see her parents. If Ben suggested taking up any more of her time Kate forced herself to refuse, to keep something of her life separate, something she could fall back on when this oddly unreal arrangement with Ben Fletcher came to an end.

She would have been very pleased with life, except for two persistent flies in the ointment. The first, and hardest to put from her mind, was her inside knowledge about Ben. To look at him was to wish it were impossible, but because the occasional friendly hug and kiss was the only physical contact he ever initiated she gradually grew resigned to the truth. And, rather to her surprise after their evening together, the second fly was Dan Beaumont. He rang her persistently, both at work and at home, and dropped in at Waverley Lodge at odd times, ostensibly to visit his grandmother, but in reality to try to convince her that she was on a losing wicket with Ben Fletcher.

During the week leading up to the Pennington hospital ball Kate vetoed the evening usually spent with Ben. All her spare time was occupied with Clare, finishing off the Carmen costume, which, according to its creator, was a knockout.

The evening before the ball Kate had a dress rehearsal in front of a full-length mirror. She shook her head, grinning at herself. What a colour scheme! On a recent weekend at home her mother had hunted out an ankle-length waist petticoat in violet satin, complete with pin-tucked flounce, once worn by Kate's great-grandmother as a bride. The scarlet satin skirt was looped up at the side over it, and Clare had hunted down a remnant of jade-green velvet for a sleeveless, tight-fitting bodice, laced together down the front with scarlet ribbons over a yellow blouse cut perilously low. Kate put a hand on one hip and struck a pose, then burst out laughing and went downstairs to show Mrs Beaumont.

Kate had purposely worked overtime beforehand so that she could take the Saturday afternoon before the ball off. She spent most of it having her long hair coaxed and teased into an improbable mass of corkscrew curls, and afterwards bought some equally improbable false eyelashes to add the finishing touch. She then rushed home to give herself plenty of time for the transfor-mation of Kate Harker, bookseller, into Carmen, the gypsy, who drove men mad with desire.

Kate giggled as she painted her legs with false tan, and sponged a little over the parts of her which showed. Of which there seemed to be a great deal too many, she thought uneasily, eyeing her rather spectacular cleavage when she was dressed. Not that she could come to much harm in company with Cassie and Alec—and Ben. She painted her eyes dramatically, then stuck on the lashes the way Emma had once taught her. She fixed a shower of gold coins to each ear, caught back her hair with a spray of artificial red roses, thrust on an armful of cheap brass bangles, fastened a gold chain round one ankle, slid her bare feet into flat black slippers, then stepped back to eye her exotic reflection.

Kate stared at the stranger in the glass with misgiving, then shrugged, picked up her wrap, and went downstairs to wait for Ben in the hall.

Ben arrived promptly as usual, looking utterly magnificent in white tie and tails, to Kate's surprise.

'Who are you supposed to be? The orchestra conductor?' she demanded, laughing. But Ben wasn't listening. He was staring at her as though he'd never seen her before.

'Hallelujah!' he breathed in awe, his eyes drinking her in from the gleaming, tousled ringlets to her black velvet toes. 'You look sensational, Kate. It *is* Kate, I assume?'

'No, it's Carmen—though only on the outside. Ben, do you think it's a bit over the top?' she asked anxiously, peering at herself in the hall mirror.

He came to stand behind her, his face intent above hers, something in his dark eyes that she'd never seen before.

'You look sexy as hell and utterly gorgeous,' he said softly, his breath brushing her ear. Suddenly he bent and pressed a kiss to her bare shoulder. 'Edible, too.' And he turned her round and bent to kiss her mouth, his grasp tightening on her elbows to bring her up on tiptoe as the kiss deepened and lengthened. He tore his mouth away at last, gazing down at her with such a desperate, questioning look that her eyes widened in alarm.

'What is it?' she asked breathlessly.

'You make it so hard for me, Kate.' He pulled her against him and held her tightly. 'I know we can never be more than good friends, but sometimes I wish like hell that things were different.'

Kate's heart gave a great sickening lurch, and she pulled away, her heart beating fast as this was the nearest Ben had ever come to confiding in her. 'It's a good thing to have friends,' she said brightly. 'I'm very lucky. I thought I was leaving my friends behind when I came to Pennington, yet I found you, Cassie and Alec. And Clare.'

He stood looking down at her, his eyes inscrutable, then he turned away, picked up the wrap and swathed her in it. 'You'll need this; it's a bit chilly tonight. *Vámonos*, Carmen, it's party time. Cassie and Alec are meeting us in the Chesterton bar, with the rest of Alec's guests. We're the only non-medics in the group.'

'Then we'll just have to stick together, won't we?' She fixed him with a militant eye as they went down the path to the Range Rover. 'You're not really going to the ball like that, Ben, are you?'

'No.' He lifted her into the passenger seat and gave her the wide white grin which never failed to make her heart turn somersaults. He nodded towards a black bundle on the back seat. 'The important bit's back there. I'll throw it on in the Chesterton car park.'

'You're determined to make me wild with curiosity right up to the last minute,' she accused. 'Does Cassie know?'

'Nope.' He smiled smugly. 'I'm good at secrets.'

Wasn't *that* the truth, thought Kate in fleeting despair.

Quarter of an hour later Ben slotted the Range Rover into a far corner of the crowded hotel car park. Giving Kate a grin, he reached behind him, shook out a black cloak lined with red satin, then fastened it on.

'I need a mirror for the next bit,' he said casually. 'Close your eyes and don't peep until I say when.'

Kate chuckled and closed her eyes obediently. 'Hurry up!' she ordered impatiently. 'I'm dying to know.'

'Right. What do you think?'

When Kate opened her eyes she found a complete stranger looking at her. A silver mask hid one side of Ben's face from the hairline of a glossy black wig to just above his jaw. She breathed out in admiration. 'Glory, Ben, how fantastic. You're the Phantom!'

'Of the opera,' he agreed smugly. 'No one stipulated which one, remember. It was Alec's talk of wigs which gave me the idea.'

'You look so different with black hair—seriously sinister. Brr!' She gave a little shiver and Ben leaned closer, his mouth brushing hers.

'I warn you, fair maiden—well, dark maiden, actually—I mean to have you in my power,' he threatened with melodrama, then laughed. 'But not before dinner. Come on, let's go.'

The staff of the Chesterton, most of them old hands, had long been inured to the spectacle of usually sober citizens transformed by gaudy costumes on the night of the hospital ball. But Kate could tell that as a couple she and Ben made quite an impression as they walked through the foyer in silence, Ben holding her by the hand. He kept her deliberately still at the entrance to the bar until Cassie, beautiful in a high-waisted black velvet gown, her hair twisted up with gold ribbons into a Grecian knot, turned to look at them and stopped what she was saying mid-sentence, her eyes like saucers as she tugged at Alec's sleeve. He turned to look and started towards them, exclaiming in surprise.

'I recognise the sexy Carmen—just—but hell, Ben, if you didn't tower over everyone as usual I'd never have known it was you.' He kissed Kate on both cheeks, clapped his brother-in-law on the back and ushered them over to join his friends. Cassie couldn't stop laughing as she looked at her disguised brother.

'Heaven knows Kate looks different enough, but that wig, Ben—what a stroke of genius!' She hugged them both, then made sure that Kate had a glass of wine and knew everyone by the time they were called in to dinner in the ballroom.

Kate had the time of her life from the word go. She was in friendly company, among people prepared to enjoy themselves to the hilt as distinguished consultants and their responsible wives let their hair down for the evening in various operatic guises, some of them easily recognisable, some of them not.

Ben, to everyone's amusement, refused to take off his mask even to eat his dinner, explaining that it was pliable enough to allow for chewing. 'Nothing comes between me and my appetite,' he said, grinning.

'We'd hoped to see you as Samson, suitably bare-chested,' said a lady dressed as Cleopatra.

'No chance,' retorted Ben, eyeing her thoughtfully. 'I don't know much about opera, Louise, but where does Cleopatra come in?'

'Aïda, of course. Oh, I know Aïda was a Nubian slave or something. Charles told me that. But who cares? I've always fancied an Egyptian costume—love the eye make-up.'

Cassie leaned across the table, smiling at Kate. 'Who did *your* make-up, love? You look so different, especially with that hair.'

Kate explained about the hairdresser who'd entered into the spirit of the thing so enthusiastically. 'She suggested the false eyelashes and I added a layer or two of paint.'

Alec patted her hand affectionately. 'You're not the only Carmen tonight, Kate, but you knock spots off all the others.'

Ben, on her other side, case her a dark look from his visible eye. 'A good thing we've got the odd heart specialist present. That neckline of, yours could cause cardiac arrest in certain quarters.'

Kate's face rivalled her scarlet satin skirt. 'It's a bit late to tell me now!'

'Ignore him,' ordered Cassie. 'You look utterly gorgeous.'

'I know she does,' said Ben bitterly. 'Trouble is, I'm not the only one. I'll be hitting callow medicos off with a stick once the music starts.'

To Kate's astonishment he was right. The moment the tables were cleared and the band in place several junior housemen came rushing to pay their respects to Mr Neville so they could ask Kate to dance. Ben solved her dilemma by telling them to run away and play for a while as Kate was dancing with him first.

'Good grief, is that you, Ben?' said a cheerful, weary-faced young man in the striped shirt and flat straw hat of a Gilbert and Sullivan gondolier. 'Didn't recognise you in the wig. Brilliant! Anyway, you can spare your Carmen for one dance, surely!'

'Possibly, but not the first one. Back off, Huxley!' Ben led Kate onto the floor, where the assembled company were doing various things to the foxtrots and quicksteps of the first half of the evening. 'Later on a rock group takes over and the younger set goes ape,' he bent to tell her.

Dancing with Ben was of necessity done mainly in silence, since the discrepancy in their respective heights made conversation impossible over the music. And since neither of them was expert at the conventional ballroom-type rhythms they soon returned to their table, which for the moment was deserted.

Ben poured more wine into Kate's glass, eyeing her questioningly. 'You're very quiet.'

'I suppose,' she said slowly, watching the dancers, 'I would have preferred to speak for myself on the subject of partners.'

Ben scowled. 'You mean you didn't want to dance with me?'

He sounded so outraged that Kate almost laughed. 'No. I didn't mean that. But, just like Dan Beaumont and his rotten Bellinis, I would have liked to be asked.'

'I apologise,' he said with cold formality, then stiffened. 'You're about to be asked now, if that suits you better. Dan done up like a dog's dinner as a matador, heaven help us.' Ben eyed the approaching figure with dislike, then turned to Kate in comprehension. 'I might have known. He's the toreador from *Carmen*, of course.'

'I didn't tell him what I'd chosen!'

Ben looked so sceptical that Kate gave Dan a rather friendlier smile than she'd intended as he arrived at the table.

Dan Beaumont, face stained dark like Kate's, in flat matador's hat, glittering beaded jacket and tight breeches, cloak slung over one shoulder, was perfect in every detail, right down to the pink stockings and pigtail of the traditional bullfighter. He swaggered up to them, obviously deeply pleased with himself.

'Hi there. Great costume, Ben.' He gave Kate a conspiratorial smile. 'What a pair we make! Dance with me?'

Kate longed to refuse, but knew there was no earthly reason why she should, and at that moment the rest of Alec's party came back to the table, there were greetings all round for Dan, and when he drew her away onto the floor there was nothing she could do but go with him.

'Clever, aren't I?' he said with satisfaction as he guided her round the floor in surprisingly expert fashion. 'I'm Escamillo, the toreador from *Carmen*. I ordered all this from London when Gran told me what you were wearing. You look surprised.'

'Not because you pumped your grandmother,' said Kate acidly, 'but because you can actually dance. You don't seem the type for strict tempo.'

'They made us learn where I went to school. Social graces and all that.' He pulled her closer, leering into the eyes only a short distance below his own. 'It has very obvious advantages.'

Kate pulled away, then wished she hadn't as his eyes dropped instantly to her neckline.

At that moment a break in the music allowed Kate to thank him for the dance and go back to the table, leaving Dan no choice but to escort her there, looking sulky.

'What's the matter?' said Ben quietly as he held out her chair for her. 'Problems?'

Kate shook her head. 'Just Dan being Dan. Is he always like this? Or only with me?'

Ben shrugged. 'He's not long out of college, had a job at the top ready and waiting when he qualified. Dan's never had to struggle for anything to date. Maybe you're the first resistance he's come up against.' His face, unreadable behind the mask, turned away slightly. 'He told me I don't stand a chance with you either.'

'What?' Kate leaned closer, frowning, so she could hear him above the music. 'Did he say why?'

'Because you failed to succumb to the Beaumont charm he's convinced you're in love with someone else.'

She sat very still. 'Oh? Who with?'

'Perhaps you'd better ask Dan that,' said Ben, then got up, holding out a hand. 'Come on, they're playing something slow. We can just sort of shuffle round the floor to this.'

He made no attempt to talk to her, merely holding her close as they moved together, and although the lights had been lowered Kate could tell they were attracting a fair amount of attention. Most people, probably, were wondering who Ben Fletcher's latest conquest was. While others who knew him better, she thought with a little shiver, might be speculating very differently.

Ben felt the shiver and drew her close, clasping her hand tightly against his chest, and Kate gave up trying to hold herself aloof. She relaxed against him on the crowded floor, giving herself up to the moment, blanking her mind against anything other than the pleasure of being in Ben's arms. When the music stopped the lights came on and she blinked owlishly up into Ben's masked face. His mouth curved in that familiar, heart-stopping smile and she smiled back, and suddenly the evening was wonderful again. There was an interval of laughter and conversation back at the table with Cassie and Alec and their friends, then shortly afterwards the band gave way to a rock group, and Kate was whisked away by Greg Huxley, gondolier-cum-junior doctor, who cheerfully promised Ben he'd bring her back in one piece.

Young Dr Huxley had cast away his straw hat, and danced with a frenzied energy that belied his exhausting work schedule, at the same time managing to carry on an animated conversation with Kate as they gyrated together.

'Actually we've met before,' shouted Kate above the music.

'Can't have. I'd have remembered.'

'I helped you find a medical textbook,' she assured him. 'I work at Hardacres.'

His freckled face looked blank. 'I can't place you—'

'I'm the one with glasses and hair screwed up in a bun.' She threw back her head and roared with laughter as comprehension dawned in Greg's eyes.

'You're kidding! Is that a wig?'

Kate shook her head, grinning. 'All mine, Doctor.'

They enjoyed the joke together, and it was with gratifying reluctance that Greg eventually let her go when she felt it was time to get back to the others.

'Ben Fletcher gets all the luck,' he said ruefully. 'Most of the young and nubile on the General nursing staff lust after him. You'd better watch your back.'

'Ben and I are just friends,' said Kate lightly, flushing at the open disbelief in the cheerful, tired eyes, and with a laugh Greg took her back to her table, exchanged some flip *badinage* with Ben, then went back to the bar.

Greg Huxley gave his colleagues the excuse they were waiting for. Kate was inundated with partners right up to the moment when the spokesman of the hospital committee thanked everyone for their support of the charity, and announced that Othello and Desdemona had won first prize for a pair, that the exotic, many-veiled

Salome was judged the best lady's costume, and the Phantom of the Opera the best male.

There was much laughter and applause as the prizes were given out, but as Ben went up to receive his trophy Kate's eyes were drawn to Dan, who was sitting with a crowd of rowdy cronies. He was staring at Ben with such open malevolence that a cold shiver ran down Kate's spine. Dan, she realised, had expected to win.

'Bloody embarrassing,' muttered Ben as he rejoined the table to a chorus of congratulations and teasing. 'I made the least effort of anyone.'

'You looked magnificent, love,' Cassie assured him. 'Though I rather think young Dan's a bit miffed his suit of lights didn't win.'

'You don't come to these things to *win*,' said Ben in disgust.

Alec laughed. 'What's your prize? A holiday in the Bahamas?'

'That'll be the day! Salome and I both got non-vintage champagne.'

Louise Conway leaned her Cleopatra headdress closer. 'Alec, you do realise who the Salome behind those veils actually is, I assume? You ought to.'

'Cassie and I were just trying to place her,' he said, then his eyes narrowed. 'Good grief! It's Sister Kenward in a yashmak and long black wig!'

Cassie gurgled in delight. 'Your theatre sister? Wonderful! I can just picture her demanding someone's head on a platter. She terrifies the junior nurses,' she added to Kate.

'And the junior doctors,' said Alec with a grin. 'She's the best in the business. I'll pull her leg on Monday!'

'Rather you than me,' said Charles Conway with feeling.

'Ah, but she eats out of Alec's hand. He's always been a wow with the female medical staff—broke hearts in all directions when he was registrar,' said Ben slyly. 'Cassie told me.'

'Did she, now?' said Alec, eyeing his wife askance.

'Well, it's true,' said Cassie, unruffled. 'I used to work at Pennington General myself, remember.' She grinned. 'He had long ringlets and an earring in those days—'

'Time we went home,' said Alec, laughing, 'before you bring up all the details of my murky past.' He turned to Ben. 'A taxi's waiting for us. Want to share it, or are you fit to drive?'

Ben looked at Kate. 'What about you? Would you like to stay? I'm happy to go now if you are—and I can pick up the car tomorrow.'

The evening was becoming a lot rowdier now that some of the older element had left. Kate nodded. 'I'm quite tired all of a sudden.'

'A pity you can't come to lunch tomorrow, Kate,' Cassie said regretfully when the taxi arrived at Beaufort Square. 'Come next Sunday instead.'

'I'd love to. And thank you for asking me to the dance tonight. It was great fun.'

'Your costume was a knockout,' said Alec, grinning. 'But the star of the evening was Sister Kenward.'

'Definitely—I can just picture her slapping scalpels into your hand,' chuckled Ben. 'Goodnight, you two. I hope Emily has a lie-in.'

There was silence in the car on the way to Waverley Lodge. It was unexpected and rather unbearable from

Kate's point of view. Something, she could tell, was bothering Ben.

'Will Mrs Beaumont object if I come in for a minute?' he asked eventually, clearing his throat. 'There's something I'd like to talk about.'

Kate bit her lip, not liking the sound of this very much. 'She went away this morning for a few days. To her brother in Chester.'

'Good.'

Ben paid off the driver then followed Kate up the path to the house. Her hand was so unsteady that in the end he took the key from her and unlocked the door himself, closing it carefully behind him once they were inside. Kate had left the lights on in her own part of the house, but the lower floor was in darkness. She reached out to turn on the hall light, but Ben took her hand, forestalling her.

'Leave it. Please.' He had taken off the mask and wig, and the upstairs landing light struck beams from his bright hair, leaving the rest of his tall figure in darkness as he looked down at her silently.

'Would you like some coffee?' asked Kate hoarsely, more to break the silence than because she thought he'd accept.

'No. I just need a talk in private. I was going to suggest we met somewhere tomorrow, but from what Cassie said you're obviously tied up then.'

'Yes. I'm spending the day with Clare.'

The silence was suddenly palpable. Ben stood like a statue, the tension in him communicating itself so clearly to Kate that she let out a choked little cry when he moved abruptly and lifted her by the elbows until she was standing on the stairs, level with him. 'Kate—' He stopped, then shrugged and pulled her close. 'Oh, hell, this is difficult. I'm trying to say it doesn't have to be like this, surely? I've never felt like this before for a woman. I can't believe you don't feel something for me too. You're so different—' He broke off, letting out a deep breath.

Different? She stood utterly still in his grasp, dizzy with hope, afraid to breathe.

'We're so good together, I just can't believe you're in love with—with someone else,' he went on huskily, his breathing quickening. 'It's new to me to have a woman as a friend. But I want more than that, Kate. I've been doing my best to be patient, but tonight, seeing you in that outfit, with guys buzzing round you like bees round a honeypot, for the first time in my life I was jealous as hell. I could have throttled Dan with my bare hands.'

Kate felt as though she was drowning in uncharted seas. The weeks of trying to accept Ben's ambivalence towards her sex had taken their toll. Was he trying to tell her that she alone, of all the women he'd known, had the power to convert him? A great surging excitement rose inside her and she leaned back against his locked hands, her eyes glittering as she gazed up into his. Wordlessly she detached herself, then turned, invitation in every line of her, and held out her hand. Ben let out a deep, unsteady breath and caught her up in his arms, leaping up the stairs with her to the dimly lit sitting room. There he set her down on her feet, breathing hard, and waited.

Shaking inside with fear and a sexual response all the more fierce for having been repressed all these weeks, Kate slowly removed her wrap, letting it fall to the floor. Ben, eyes burning darkly in a suddenly pale face, took off his theatrical cape and stripped off the coat beneath it. He undid his tie and threw it down, then came to her and drew her close.

Her heart hammered against the velvet bodice as he bent to kiss her. He laid one long hand flat at the base of her spine to pull her against him. Kate felt the blood rush to her face at the contact. He wanted her! Exultation opened her mouth as his tongue came seeking, and suddenly they were breathing like long-distance runners, his fingers were pulling apart the ribbons of her bodice, pushing the blouse away, and she was tugging at his shirt, desperate to feel skin against skin. She tugged off the earrings and bangles and Ben tore the flowers from her hair. They sank to their knees together, kissing wildly as he got rid of his shirt and pulled her against him, and the breath left her in a rush as they lay full length. Her hips thrust against him and he groaned, and his mouth tore away from hers, but only to cause havoc elsewhere, until her entire body became liquid with welcome, melting in the crucible of feeling that Ben, it was triumphantly obvious, was experiencing as violently as she.

With shaking hands he removed the rest of her finery, then looked deep into her eyes.

'Tell me the truth, Kate,' he said, breathing hard. 'Do you want this?'

'You know I do,' she said fiercely, pulling him down to her. 'Don't talk. Love me.'

Ben kissed her like a man starved, his lips bruising hers, his tongue seeking out the contours of her open, willing mouth, as he stripped off the last of his clothes. He broke away for a moment and, eyes closed, her heart hammering, Kate waited for what seemed an eternity.

Surely he wouldn't be cruel enough to change his mind now? she thought in agony, then let out a long, sobbing gasp as he lifted her hips and vanquished her doubts with one powerful thrust of his body.

A powerful sense of utter rightness filled Kate as Ben made love to her. This was what she'd been born for—this mounting heat and passion, the ravishing combination of ferocity and tenderness that Ben brought to their loving. He smiled down into her eyes, unhurried and relishing the moment at first, then, as his own urges began to master him, the rhythm grew faster and less controlled until they were caught up together in a headlong, mutual rush to achieve the culmination which overwhelmed them both in gasping, heart-thudding triumph.

CHAPTER NINE

THEY lay tangled together, eyes closed, arms fast about each other, until their heart rates slowed and breathing was no longer a painful exercise. Kate felt bereft and cold as Ben pulled away at last and left the room. She opened one eye slightly, saw a drift of red satin and pulled it over herself, wondering what to do next. Then Ben returned, tossed away her impromptu quilt and scooped her up in his arms.

'Let's go to bed,' he said, solving her problem.

Close in Ben's arms under the covers, Kate, exhausted but crazily happy, gave silent thanks to Mrs Beaumont for providing her with a double bed, instead of the narrow single of her flat-sharing days.

'Ben,' she said drowsily as he stroked her hair back from her forehead, 'what about Griff?'

He kissed her nose. 'Thoughtful girl. He's with my neighbours upstairs until tomorrow.'

Kate drew away, staring into the relaxed, handsome face so close to hers. 'You mean you anticipated all this?'

Ben nipped her earlobe with his teeth in rebuke. 'No, I did not! It was just too long to leave the dog on his own tonight. You're not thinking straight. I didn't know Mrs Beaumont was away. The most I'd hoped for was to ask you to come round to my place tomorrow, if only for a few minutes. I had something to ask.'

'What was it?'

'The question wasn't necessary. What happened between us just now answered it without words.' Ben closed her eyes with his lips. 'Sleep now. Talk later.'

Kate had never actually slept with a man before. Curiosity had led her into a couple of love affairs in college because everyone else was doing the same. But the encounters merely convinced her that the whole thing was much overrated, and something she could happily do without, which meant that her more recent friendships with men had been short-lived, mainly because none of the men in question shared her outlook on sex. With Ben she had been the one irked by a platonic relationship. Now everything was different. Utterly transformed. But she was too tired to worry about it. With a sigh she nestled closer and Ben's embrace tightened in reassurance. Curled close against his long, muscular body, Kate drifted into sleep.

She woke to a wonderful sensation of security, still clasped in Ben's arms. She gazed at the beautiful male face on the pillow beside her, hardly able to believe that he was actually here in her bed. He was sound asleep, the bright hair damp and tangled on his forehead, his broad chest rising and falling against her with relaxed regularity. Kate lay very still, her mind trying to grasp this new, incredible turn of events. Was this the first time Ben had made love to a woman? If so he was remarkably expert.

She made herself examine the idea. Last night she hadn't given Ben's secret life a thought. From the moment they'd arrived back from the ball things had been very different between them. Her eyes narrowed as she remembered Ben's kiss when he'd come to collect her. It had started then. Ben had found her desirable in her gypsy finery. And out of it, too, she thought, heat rushing all over her body, communicating itself to the man holding her so possessively close. Ben's eyes opened on her flushed face, blinked, then lit up with such smouldering male need that she melted against him and he crushed her close, kissing her hungrily, caressing her with intent, relentless skill, until at last she was breathless and pleading and consumed by a need as fierce as his.

'Now we talk,' said Ben a long, long time later.

Kate felt a cold chill of apprehension. 'Do we?'

'Where are you going today?'

'To lunch with Clare.'

Ben's face darkened and he pulled her close. 'Ring her and cancel. Tell her you're ill. Or, better still, tell her the truth.'

Kate raised herself on one elbow to look down into his face. 'What truth is that?'

'That you'd rather be with me. I'll send out for a meal.'

Sorely tempted, Kate sighed and shook her head. 'Ben, I can't. I promised. And Clare was so good, making the costume for me. Besides, I'm very fond of her—'

'So I hear,' he said coldly.

She stared at him. 'I'm sorry?'

'Not as sorry as me,' he said, sliding from the bed. 'I'd better get dressed.'

'Ben! What is this? You knew I was tied up today.'

He left without answering, and Kate jumped out of bed, shrugging into her yellow robe. She marched into the sitting room, where Ben was pulling on his clothes.

'What's the matter?' she demanded.

He buttoned his shirt swiftly, his face coldly hostile. 'I was fool enough to think that after last night—and this morning—things would be different.'

'They are,' she said vehemently. 'Vastly different.'

'But not different enough.' He slid his feet into his shoes. 'With typical male vanity, I took it for granted that once you'd made love with me that would be enough.'

'Enough for what?' she said, mystified.

Ben shrugged on his coat and picked up the cape. 'If you have to ask, Kate, there's not much point in explaining.' He picked up the phone. 'All right if I ring for a cab? I don't fancy walking through Pennington in this gear.'

'Of course.' Kate turned on her heel and ran to the bathroom, trying to hold back her tears. What in the world was wrong with Ben? She swallowed hard, dragged a brush through her hair then went out onto the landing to see Ben in the hall below, watching for the taxi. His eyes lit up as he looked up at her.

'You've changed your mind?'

Kate blinked hard. 'I can't, Ben. I *promised*,' she said miserably.

'Pity.' He shrugged. 'No matter. I'll go home and walk Griff, then go off to the gym. A good workout usually cures most ills where I'm concerned.'

'Ah, yes, your club. I'm sure you'll find all kinds of solace there,' she said bitingly, suddenly so angry that she could have thrown something at him.

Ben came to the foot of the stairs, his eyes suddenly menacing. 'What the hell do you mean by that?'

Kate shrugged disdainfully. 'Just what I said.'

His jaw tightened. 'As it happens Sunday afternoons are men-only sessions.'

'Just as I thought,' she snapped, and went into her bedroom and slammed the door.

Ben was halfway up the stairs after her when the doorbell rang. He stopped, and she waited in an agony of anticipation, but in the end he went down again, opened the front door and closed it behind him with a crash that shook the little house, and Kate threw herself face down on the bed and gave way to bitter tears all the more painful because the pillow retained Ben's warmth and the fresh, tangy scent of his skin, flooding her with a feeling of unbearable loss after the rapture she'd experienced at his hands so short a time before. Life was a cruel see-saw, she thought bitterly. Last night she'd been high in the clouds. Today she was back down to earth again with a vengeance.

Clare and Robert Payne lived on the outskirts of Pennington in a small, pretty cottage, crowded on this occasion with guests invited to celebrate the Paynes' tenth anniversary. Kate was plied with delicious buffet food and given such a warm welcome that it almost convinced her she'd been right to say no to Ben, despite his angry exit. But no welcome in the world, other than Ben's open arms, could begin to make up for the misery she was doing her best to hide under a bright smile as she gave Clare a quick account of the ball.

Kate stuck it out for as long as possible, but left fairly early, worn out by keeping up the pretence of vivacity. When she got back to Waverley Lodge her phone was ringing. She sprinted up the stairs and snatched up the receiver, trembling with hope.

'Kate? It's Cassie.'

Kate slumped to the floor in despair. 'Hi, Cassie. How are you after the excitement of last night? Did Emily give you a lie-in?'

'No such luck. But she's gone down now, thank goodness. You haven't seen Ben by any chance, have you?'

If only she had! 'No. I've just come in from a lunch party at Clare Payne's house. Why? Were you expecting him?'

'Not really. My mother's been trying to ring him. No success, so she rang me.'

'Doesn't he go to the gym on Sundays?'

'I tried there but nobody's seen him today. It's after seven, Kate. I'm worried. If Ben contacts you will you tell him to ring Mother first and then me?'

'Yes, of course.' Kate cleared her throat. 'But I don't think Ben *will* ring me.'

'Why? Have you two fallen out?'

'Yes. Badly.'

'Funny! You looked very much in tune last night. What happened?'

'He was angry because I wouldn't cancel lunch with Clare.'

'Is *that* all? Doesn't sound like Ben!'

'True, though.' Kate knuckled a tear away drearily. 'Oh, by the way, Cassie, Clare's over the moon. She's expecting a baby. Today is her tenth anniversary—apparently she'd almost given up hope.'

'How lovely! Congratulate her for me.' Cassie paused. 'Look, Kate, tell me to mind my own business if you like, but are you all right? You sound very unhappy.'

Longing to sob out her hurt and misery, Kate tried to reassure Cassie, then, unable to trust her voice any longer, put down the phone and sat with her head in her hands. Where on earth was Ben? She wanted to see him so much it was a physical ache. Like Ben, she'd thought last night had changed everything. But it obviously hadn't for him. Not in the same way. There were men, she knew, who could relate to either sex. Yet last night, this morning too, Ben had made her feel that his love-making arose not only from sheer urgent male need but from a need which she alone could satisfy.

Next day Kate's job was more irksome than usual, but it had one benefit. Clare had taken a few days off, which meant that Kate had too much to do to spare time for agonising over Ben. Mrs Harrison helped out by taking over at lunch, but for the rest of the day Kate worked like a demon, missing Clare's banter. She drove Harry and Gail hard, and the part-timers taken on to fill the gap were run off their feet to meet her demands. At any other time she might have been more lenient, but she felt at odds with the world all day, and was heartily glad when it was time to shut up shop and go off to her evening class.

The evenings were light enough now to make the walk home afterwards pleasant, and, ignoring her aching feet, Kate walked briskly back to Waverley Lodge. But when she unlocked the door her heart sank. Dan sauntered out of his grandmother's sitting room, a mocking smile on his thin, self-confident face.

'Only me, Kate.'

She stared at him coldly, leaving the door deliberately ajar as a hint to speed him on his way. 'So I see.'

'Just came to check everything's OK.'

'Did you?' she said stonily. 'Why?'

Dan came towards her. 'Why the hell are you so hostile, Kate?'

'I'm not. Just indifferent,' she added, shrugging, and Dan coloured angrily.

'I could change that,' he assured her, an ugly look in his eyes. 'Don't try to come the prim and proper miss after wearing that sexy little outfit to the dance. I could soon have you begging for it!'

Kate sighed, looking deliberately bored. 'Oh, please! Try to be original at least.'

Dan moved like lightning, seizing her in his arms and grinding his mouth into hers, but Kate bit his lip so savagely that he let out a grunt of pain, momentarily loosening his hold. She took advantage of it, racing up the stairs, with Dan in hot pursuit, howling with pain. Halfway up he caught her by the belt of her raincoat, and Kate wrenched round to hit him, sending them both off balance. She lost her footing, and tumbled downstairs with a scream, sprawling, winded, on the hall carpet.

Dan came racing down after her, seizing her hand, calling her name in shrill panic, but Kate lay deliberately still, eyes closed, wanting to scare him witless. Let him think he'd done some serious damage, she thought malevolently.

Dan was panting and moaning, trying to find the pulse in her wrist, then he breathed in sharply, and Kate opened one eye a crack to see Dan staring up in horror at the tall, unmistakable figure in the open doorway.

'What the hell—?' Ben brushed Dan aside as if he were a fly, and fell to his knees beside Kate.

'What the devil have you done to her, Beaumont?' he demanded, in a tone so deadly quiet that Dan's face took on a greenish pallor as he dabbed at his bleeding, swollen lip.

'I haven't done anything—she tripped and fell down the stairs. Shall I ring for an ambulance?'

Kate felt it was time to open her eyes, and found Ben's staring down into hers, an odd twist to his mouth. 'Hello,' he said quietly. 'Lie still. I'm just going to check for broken bones.' He ran his hands over her, but, as Kate could have told him, nothing was wrong.

'My head,' she moaned artistically.

Ben picked her up and sat her on Mrs Beaumont's settle. 'I'd better take you to Casualty.'

Dan gave a muffled groan. 'I'm sorry, Kate. I never meant to hurt you.'

'Just go away and leave me alone,' she snapped.

Dan winced and stood erect, facing Ben defiantly. 'It wasn't my fault.'

'Is that true?' Ben asked Kate.

'He didn't push me down the stairs,' she said scrupulously. 'But I only ran up there to get away from him. He was all over me like an octopus—had some idea of making me beg for it. That's right, isn't it, Dan? I believe those were your words. I bit him, ran upstairs, and he followed and caught me. I pulled free and tumbled down like Jack, and broke my crown.'

Ben turned to Dan Beaumont with a look which brought perspiration out in beads on the other man's forehead. 'I wish I could thump the living daylights out of you to teach you a lesson. But I can't because I'm twice your size and you happen to be your father's son.'

'Afraid to lose your job!' sneered Dan, licking dry lips.

'I think that's pretty unlikely—'

'Don't be too sure!'

Ben eyed him coldly. 'Get out of here, Dan. And take my advice: leave Kate alone in future.'

'Or what, eunuch?' said Dan, then let out a yelp as Ben abruptly picked him up by the scruff of his neck and threw him out of the house.

'Gosh!' said Kate in admiration. 'I wish I could have done that.'

'Come on,' said Ben. 'I'm taking you to Casualty.'

'There's no need—honestly,' she confessed. 'I didn't hurt myself when I fell. I put on an act to frighten Dan.'

'Are you sure?' he demanded.

'I bruised my knee a bit, but otherwise I'm fine.' Kate sighed. 'But I'll have to find another flat. I'm fond of Mrs Beaumont, but I can't be doing with her grandson.'

'You could move in with me,' said Ben casually.

Kate's heart gave a thump. 'What—what did you say?'

'You heard me. I said come and live with me,' he repeated.

She stared at him, dumbfounded, then breathed in deeply. 'I need some tea.'

Ben locked the front door then followed Kate upstairs, leaning in the kitchen doorway as he watched her fill the kettle and set a tray. 'My offer obviously comes as a shock,' he remarked casually.

Kate threw him a far from friendly look. 'Does that surprise you, Ben? You went off in a rage yesterday morning, remember? Where did you go? Cassie rang here looking for you.'

'I drove Griff down to Broadway and walked miles with him. I had dinner in a pub on the way back and got home rather late to a lot of phone messages.' He looked at her steadily. 'None of them from you.'

Kate's mouth tightened. 'Did you expect one?'

'No. I spent the entire day trying to come to terms with a lot of things. By the time I got back I suppose I hoped you'd have rung.'

Her eyes flashed. 'So why didn't you ring me?'

'It was late. I thought you might be asleep.'

Kate raised a cynical eyebrow and bent to look in her fridge. 'Would you like something to eat? I don't have much in here. Not that I'm hungry.'

Ben frowned. 'Did you eat lunch?'

'No, I was too busy. Clare's on holiday.'

'Ah, yes. Clare.' He closed the space between them, put a finger under her chin and raised her face to his. 'I need to talk to you, which is why I came round in the first place. But it's late and I'm hungry.' He smiled down at her, and unwillingly Kate smiled back.

'I can make you an omelette.'

Ben nodded with enthusiasm. 'Done. But only if you eat one too, Kate.'

In minutes they were making inroads on the quickly prepared meal, Kate finding she was hungry after all.

'I feel better,' she admitted afterwards.

'I thought you would,' he said smugly, starting on a plate of cheese and biscuits. 'You need taking care of, my girl.'

'I do not! I'm perfectly capable of looking after myself—'

'So I saw when I arrived tonight!'

They glared at each other, then Ben's face softened into the grin which never failed to work its magic on Kate. She laughed, shrugging.

'All right. I'll admit Dan took me by surprise. But now I've calmed down I'm not going to let him chase me away from this place.'

'Not even to move in with me?' he said promptly.

'Not even to do that,' she returned. 'I've never lived with a man yet. One way and another you and I don't know each other well enough to set up house together.'

'Even if I said you could occupy my spare bedroom?'

Kate's eyes narrowed. 'Is that what you had in mind?'

Ben scowled. 'You know damn well it isn't. But if that's what you'd prefer—to start with, anyway—then I'd be noble and give you a bed to yourself. For a while.'

'Have you ever lived with a woman, Ben? Apart from your mother, I mean,' asked Kate, staring down into her cup.

'Yes. Once.' He grinned. 'The house had low beams and the rooms were small. In the end I had to leave for the sake of sheer self-preservation.'

There was a silence for a moment. 'Would you like a drink?' asked Kate at last, aware that Ben was watching her.

'No, thanks. I haven't had this talk yet, remember.'

'Let me make you some coffee, then—'

Kate half rose, but Ben got up and pushed her back on the sofa, seating himself beside her. He slid an arm behind her and drew her close.

'Forget the coffee. I think it's time to tell you exactly who Dan said you were in love with, Kate. I flatly refused to believe him, but he's a cunning little swine. Told me his grandmother let him know in confidence. He was full of admiration because old Mrs Beaumont was so broad-minded.'

Kate twisted round to look up at him, frowning. 'Broad-minded?'

Ben nodded, grasping her hand in his as he looked deliberately round the room.

'What's the matter?' she demanded irritably. 'For heaven's sake, Ben, get on with it.'

'I was just making sure no missiles were within reach,' he said, grinning.

'Ben Fletcher, tell me who the mystery lover is or I'll scream!'

His eyes locked with hers. 'Dan said the only reason he couldn't get to first base with you was your lack of interest in men. He swore you were in love with Clare.'

CHAPTER TEN

KATE stared up at Ben, dumbfounded. 'You're joking!' she said incredulously.

He shook his head. 'That's what the man said.'

'And you believed him?'

'No, of course I didn't. Not at first, anyway.' Ben's jaw tightened. 'But all you seemed to want from me was friendship, and in the end I began to think, just as Dan intended, that a relationship with me might well be a convenient cover for the one he said you had with Clare. One which might not go down well with the Hardacres management.'

'But Clare's *married*!'

'I know.' Ben's face flushed a little. 'But that's not unusual for either sex. And you spend a hell of a lot of time with her.'

Kate detached herself from him firmly and curled up in the corner of the sofa, consumed with a burning desire to murder Dan Beaumont. 'Normally I go to the cinema with her once a week at the most. But lately she's been making my costume for the ball so I've been at her house a lot more than usual. How she'd laugh if she knew!' She frowned suddenly. 'But wait a minute. You obviously don't believe all that rubbish any more.' What changed your mind?'

'Cassie told me why you went to Clare's yesterday.' Ben grimaced. 'You didn't say it was a party. When you insisted on going to Clare instead of staying with me

143

after the night we'd spent I couldn't take it. I'm human, Kate.'

'Did Cassie mention that Clare's pregnant, too?' asked Kate coolly. 'That after trying for years she's finally going to give her husband the child they've longed for?'

Ben winced. 'Yes,' he admitted stiffly.

'Hah! That's what really convinced you. Why couldn't you have been honest and just asked me, Ben?'

He stared at her scornfully. 'Oh, come on, Kate! How the hell could I ask a girl a question like that?'

Kate looked at the brooding, spectacularly handsome face, feeling a shiver run down her spine. Dan Beaumont had obviously lied about Ben too.

'Ben,' she said hesitantly, 'will you promise to keep your cool if I ask *you* a very personal question?'

He relaxed slightly. 'I'll try, Kate. Ask on.'

'The other night...' she began, then turned away to avoid his eyes. 'The other night,' she continued doggedly, 'it was pretty obvious you'd made love before. A lot.'

Ben laughed involuntarily. 'Hell, Kate, I'm thirty-one. What did you expect?'

Which was only half the answer Kate wanted.

'What's the matter?' he asked indulgently. 'Do you want a list of names?'

It was exactly what Kate wanted, but there was no way she could say so. She pulled a face and said nothing, and Ben grinned and settled down lower in his corner of the sofa.

'As I said before, when I went to college it was like being let loose in the candy store. But after a while I put on the brakes and reminded myself I was there to get a degree. So I tried monogamy and went steady with Sam for a while.'

Sam? Kate stiffened.

'What's the matter now?' he asked quickly.

'Nothing. Carry on.'

Ben eyed her questioningly, shrugged, and went on with his list. 'I found monogamy hard, but luckily so did Sam. So we broke up. The next relationship was a touch dangerous. I learnt a lot, but it nearly put paid to my college career.'

'Why?'

'I, er, caught the eye of my tutor's partner. The tutor objected violently, and who could blame him? Adele was drop-dead gorgeous, a mature, sexy woman who taught me a lot—' He broke off. 'What's the matter?'

Kate took a deep breath. 'Ben. There's something I've got to tell you. Dan spread his poison in my direction too.' She swallowed. 'He warned me not to get involved because—because your success with women was just a smokescreen . . . that you preferred men,' she finished in a rush, her face scarlet.

'What?' Ben shot bolt upright, rigid with anger. 'And you actually believed him?'

Kate bit her lip in misery. 'I didn't want to, but I had no way of finding out if he was right. I could hardly ask Cassie, could I?'

'So why the hell did you go on seeing me?' demanded Ben furiously.

'For the same reason, presumably, that you went on seeing me,' she retorted, no longer meek. 'I know—and like—several people who prefer their own sex, Ben. I count them among my friends.' She shrugged. 'So if friendship was the only thing on offer from you I wanted it.'

'I could murder Dan Beaumont!' said Ben explosively, and jumped to his feet, thrusting a hand through his hair. 'Though you're wrong about the friendship bit where I was concerned. Once I got to know you I just couldn't believe I wouldn't make you want me the same way I wanted you. I was sure we'd be lovers eventually. And I was right. The other night I proved it beyond all doubt—'

'Is that what you were doing?' she demanded wrathfully. 'Proving a point?'

'No, it damn well wasn't—and even if I was it seems you were doing the same!' His eyes glittered malevolently. 'Evil little creep, I'll pulverise him—'

'You can't do that, remember,' she pointed out swiftly.

Ben calmed down a little. 'You're right, of course,' he said bitterly. 'I owe a lot to George Beaumont. His firm sponsored me through college.'

'So what possessed Dan to make such mischief?' asked Kate.

'Jealousy. He fancied you. He's been spoilt, always had everything he wanted. He couldn't take it when it seemed you preferred my company to his.'

'Right,' she said ruefully. 'I tried not to, but I couldn't help it.'

Ben's eyes softened and he sat down again, taking her hand in his. 'Even after Dan's lies?'

'I won't say I was overjoyed when he told me. But it made no difference. Once I'd found out you weren't Cassie's husband, anyway!'

'Lord, yes. I had that hurdle to get over first as well.' He moved nearer. 'So you liked me.'

'Yes. So much that I almost convinced myself I could be satisfied with just friendship,' she said honestly. 'But it made me a bit depressed at times, especially when I was with Cassie and the baby, not to mention Angus.'

'Why then particularly?'

Kate hesitated, then looked at him squarely. 'You put me off any other man's company. Which, one way and another, made babies of my own a bit unlikely.'

Ben looked at her in silence for so long that she began to fidget. 'I see a lot of things now,' he said musingly. 'Your reaction when I mentioned Sam, for one. Who, by the way, is a blonde junior barrister married to her pupil-master.'

She grinned. 'I'm glad. But no more names, please— the list's bound to be yards long, for that face of yours alone.'

'The alone bit is interesting.' He smiled. 'Are you im- plying some women might even notice the brain behind it?'

'I couldn't care less about other women—'

'Me neither,' he said swiftly, and pulled her onto his lap, staring straight into her eyes. 'Are you looking, Kate Harker? What do you see in my eyes?'

'Me,' she said slowly, her colour rising.

Ben nodded, his eyes still locked with hers. 'Doesn't that tell you something?'

Kate's eyes closed involuntarily, but she could still see the intent, handsome face, limned behind her lids, etched on her mind's eye. Then his mouth met hers, possessive and utterly irresistible, and she melted against him, hands and mouth as urgent as his. But after a while, to her intense disappointment, Ben raised his head and held her cradled against his shoulder, making no move to carry her to bed.

'I wish I could say I wanted you from the first,' said Ben musingly, stroking her hair. 'But I didn't. Actually you got me on the raw, freezing me with the icy disapproval behind those famous glasses of yours.'

Kate chuckled, pushing her tumbled hair back from her face. 'Cassie hinted I could make more of myself than my workaday persona.'

'Don't!' said Ben sharply. 'Keep to the bun and the glasses, please.' He kissed her mouth lingeringly. 'I want copyright on the falling-down hair and the wanton look.'

She smiled up at him dreamily. 'I was pretty miserable when you stormed out of here yesterday.'

'So was I.' Ben rubbed his cheek against her hair. 'It was a kick in the teeth—'

'To your ego?'

He shook her slightly. 'No. To my feelings. Not that we've discussed feelings yet—yours or mine.'

'I said I liked you,' she pointed out.

Ben grimaced. 'So you did. But you like Griff too.'

'Wrong. I adore Griff!' Kate's eyes danced as she smiled up at him, but won no answering smile from Ben.

'As I've told you before, Kate, you're different from all the other women I've known. Not *quite* as different as Dan said, thank God,' he added, the smile returning. 'What happened between us after the ball was a pretty unbelievable experience.'

'For me too,' she said with feeling. 'I had no idea it could be like that.'

He laughed a little. 'But then, both of us thought we'd achieved a miracle!'

'We did,' said Kate softly, and reached up to kiss him. 'It was miraculous for me, anyway.'

'All the more reason to come and live with me,' he said urgently. 'My flat's big enough for two.'

Kate was sorely tempted, but in the end she shook her head. 'Don't stalk off in a temper again, Ben,' she implored, 'but could you let me get used to the idea first, before I burn my boats and say yes?'

His eyes were hard to read. 'If that's what you want, then yes, Kate, I'll wait. But not for long.'

'What does that mean?' she demanded angrily. 'That if I hang about too long the offer may not still be open?'

'No, dammit. I meant that I'll keep after you until you give in.' He gave her a long, steady look. 'My powers of persuasion can be pretty formidable when I want something as much as this.'

But what was 'this'? thought Kate, her eyes troubled. As she looked into the masculine beauty of Ben Fletcher's face, it was hard to deny him anything. But events had moved so fast lately that she needed time to adjust, to get used to the idea of sharing her life with Ben. She wanted to. Oh, *how* she wanted to. But not yet.

Ben was as good as his word. He soon made sure that everyone of their acquaintance knew they were officially a pair. He called at the shop to take her out to lunch, often waited to take her home in the evenings, and made it plain that he expected all her social time to be reserved for him alone, other than Sundays with the Nevilles and the one evening a week she spent with Clare at the cinema. Ben was no cinema fan, so this worked well.

When Kate found out that her exam results were good he took her out to celebrate at the Brasserie in Sussex

Gardens, proving to her that it wasn't the surroundings, or the food, but the company which counted most for a happy evening. With Ben the dinner seemed delicious, the wine perfect, and the fact that several friends acknowledged her escort seemed only right and natural, since they made the first move and not he.

But Ben made no attempt to take her to bed again. Once Mrs Beaumont was back there was no way Kate felt she could ask him to stay the night. But although they often ate supper together at his flat, and went back there sometimes on Sunday, he didn't take her to bed there either. He kissed her and caressed her until they were both crazy with frustration, but told her quite bluntly that until she said yes to the move this was all there would be.

Kate would have been angry if Ben hadn't assured her bitterly that it was a hell of a sight more frustrating for a mere male animal like him. He made no attempt to hide how much he wanted her, and both infuriated and impressed her with his iron will-power. It was blackmail of a kind, but it made no difference to their growing closeness in every other aspect of their relationship.

Then Kate decided to go home to Guildford and her parents one weekend, and, despite Ben's request, insisted on going alone.

'I'd like to meet your parents, Kate,' he told her as they sat in the car outside the Lodge after an evening out together.

'Certainly not,' she said flatly. 'Once they lay eyes on you they'll think the worst.'

'The worst being what exactly?' he demanded, frowning.

'Wedding bells,' she said succinctly. 'So you stay here and I'll go there. See you Monday.'

'I thought you were coming back on Sunday night!'

Kate informed him that she always came back with the first train on Monday. 'Otherwise it's not worth going.'

'If I went too I could drive you down and you'd have even more time,' he pointed out.

She shook her head. 'Next time, maybe. The thing is, Ben,' she added honestly, 'you're so damnably good-looking. One look at you would convince my mother I was head over heels in love with you and the next minute she'd be writing out guest-lists.' She pulled a face. 'No way.'

'I wish you were,' he said, taking her in his arms.

'What?'

'Head over heels in love with me.' Ben kissed her long and hard, then leaned over, undid her seatbelt and ran a hand over his hair. 'All right. You win—this time. But next time,' he added menacingly, '*I* will.'

Kate spent a pleasant weekend, enjoying the spoiling she received from both parents, and returned early on Monday, certain she'd see Ben at lunchtime. Her dis-appointment when he didn't come for her was so bitter that she had to work hard to hide it. When she locked the shop that night Ben wasn't there waiting to take her home either, and there were tears in her eyes as she hurried back to Waverley Lodge. She came out of the bath to answer the phone half an hour later, her eyes like stars when she heard Ben's voice.

'I've been to London today, Kate—just got in. Come and have dinner with me?'

'Where?'

'Here. If you call a cab I'll have time to make myself presentable by the time you get here.'

Kate set out on foot, and enjoyed the walk, glad she'd decided to dispense with a taxi. The evening was fine, with a brisk breeze chasing the setting sun, and after their short separation she was filled with anticipation at the thought of seeing Ben again. She dawdled a little, enjoying the anticipation, and when she reached Ben's flat he swept her inside, crushing her to him with a kiss which went on and on until neither of them could breathe.

'What took you so long?' he demanded, and fell to kissing her again before she could answer.

'I walked,' she gasped, pushing him away a little. 'And I had to dry my hair a bit first. I was in the bath when you rang.'

'I missed you like hell,' he informed her, and opened the kitchen door to let an ecstatic Griff hurl himself at Kate. It was some time, one way and another, before she noticed that there was no sign of food anywhere.

'Would you consider it unromantic, Ben Fletcher, if I said I was hungry?' she said, laughing. 'I've been working hard today. Where's this dinner you promised?'

Ben shut the door on a doleful Griff and led Kate into his large sitting room, glancing at his watch. 'By the time you've munched on some of those nuts it should be here.'

Which it was. Right on cue a local catering firm delivered salmon *en croute*, a crisp green salad, and a strawberry mousse for pudding.

'Goodness,' said Kate in awe as she began the meal. 'Is this a celebration?'

'I'll tell you later.' Ben smiled enigmatically and fell to on the meal, asking her about her weekend and telling her what he'd done with his. 'Odd, really,' he said, helping himself to more salad. 'I was restless at Cassie's yesterday. Even Angus commented on it.'

'Why?'

'You know damn well why! I've eaten Sunday lunch with Cassie pretty often since Mother married Mike, but yesterday I missed having you there. As my sister pointed out.'

Kate was deliriously happy to hear it. She smiled radiantly at Ben and admitted that she'd missed him too. When the meal was over Ben picked her up and sat with her on the sofa, kissing and caressing her until it took every ounce of self-control she possessed not to beg him to take her to bed.

'I'm still waiting for you to say yes to the move, Kate,' he said raggedly after a while. 'But while you were away it dawned on me why you were hanging back. I realised what an idiot I'd been not to do something about it before.'

Kate looked up at him questioningly, and Ben set her on her feet. 'Stay there for a moment. I brought you a present from London.'

Kate stood in the middle of the room, wondering what Ben meant. She heard him laugh, then some scuffling and commands to Griff as the dog came loping into the room, a small paper bag in his mouth. Griff laid it on the floor in front of Kate then stood, tail wagging, waiting for the praise and thanks she lavished on him. She picked up the bag and took out a small box, her smile fading as she met Ben's eyes.

'Is this my present?'

He nodded. 'Open it.'

Kate snapped open the small leather box and bit her bottom lip in dismay. The gold ring inside was set with a ruby flanked by two smaller diamonds.

'You don't like it?' demanded Ben.

'It's—beautiful.' Kate licked suddenly dry lips and stared at him imperiously. 'Ben, is this what you meant? The way to persuade me to move in? You thought I was dragging my feet to force a proposal?'

'Force?' he said hotly. 'What the hell are you talking about? When you mentioned wedding bells the penny dropped. I thought you meant you needed commitment from me before burning your boats. Your phrase, not mine,' he reminded her.

Kate closed the small box very carefully, put it back in the bag and held it out. 'Sorry, Ben.'

His eyes glittered angrily. 'What do you mean?'

'I mean I'm sorry you thought I was holding out for a ring. I wasn't. And frankly,' she added, suddenly losing her temper, 'it's a damned insult. I was ready to come to you tonight and say, Right, I'm ready; I'll move in whenever you want. All I needed was a little time to get used to the idea, not an expensive bribe. You actually thought I was dragging my heels just to railroad you into buying me this? Thanks a lot!' She shuddered and dropped the package on the table, then stalked past him into the hall to pick up the phone.

Ben seized her from behind, his fingers bruising her elbows. 'Where the hell do you think you're going?'

'Take your hands away,' she said, so coldly that he obeyed out of sheer surprise. 'I'm just calling a taxi.'

'I'll drive you home,' he said flatly, and took the phone from her.

'As you wish.'

The drive back was completed in stony silence. When they reached Waverley Lodge Ben killed the engine and turned in his seat to look at her.

'I'd hoped the evening would end in bed,' he said, brutally blunt. 'I forced myself to wait because this time, I told myself—bloody fool that I am—it was going to be different. I don't know what it is you have that the others don't, Kate, but just for the record it's something I wanted on a permanent, committed basis. The ring was meant as a symbol of why I made myself wait until we were sharing our lives, instead of just a bed now and then.'

'You might have told me,' she said rashly. 'I'd begun to wonder if what Dan said was right, after all.'

Ben gave her a look of such utter distaste that she went cold. He got out of the car, walked round it unhurriedly to help her down, his face as blank and beautiful as a Greek statue's as he escorted her punctiliously to the door, then turned on his heel and without a word went back to the car. The look in his eyes stayed with Kate all that long, sleepless night as she tried, unsuccessfully, to convince herself that she'd done the right thing. Ben was in the wrong. He'd made her feel cheap, as though she'd demanded the ring as the price of her consent. But she'd had the last word. She shuddered at the memory of it, desperately afraid that it was the last word she'd ever say to Ben. After tonight he would probably never want to lay eyes on her again.

CHAPTER ELEVEN

ANY self-respecting tragedy queen, thought Kate as the days went by, would lose weight, look ethereally fragile. Instead she took comfort in chocolate biscuits and the cakes Gail's mother regularly provided for coffee-breaks, ate calorie-laden snacks at night instead of her usual salads, and never lost an ounce. On the other hand, she found, surprised, she didn't gain ounces either. Misery, it seemed, burned off more calories than bliss.

Since it was obvious to all concerned that a tall, striking escort no longer took her to lunch or drove her home at night Kate made a concise statement in the staffroom that she was no longer seeing Ben Fletcher. Not in the flesh, anyway, she thought miserably. Otherwise his face came between her eyes and the television screen, the books she read, and she fancied she saw that bright, sun-streaked head above the crowd everywhere she went. But he could have vanished off the face of the earth for all she actually did see of him.

After two weeks of taut, controlled despair Kate asked for leave and went home to her parents, thanking her lucky stars that she'd refused to take Ben with her on her previous visit. This way there was no surprise when she announced that she'd broken up with her current boyfriend. It had happened often enough before.

While she was in Guildford Kate went up to London, looked up Emma and Liz and stayed the weekend, trying hard to join in when the girls invited people in for an impromptu party. She returned to Pennington in a heat-wave at last, determined to apply for a transfer within Hardacres.

The Nevilles had taken the children to stay with their grandparents by the sea in Wales for a couple of weeks shortly after Kate's parting with Ben, which meant that more than a month had elapsed since that fateful Monday night before Kate had a telephone call from a deeply disturbed Cassie.

'They told me in the shop you were away, Kate. What's all this with you and Ben?' she demanded once the pre-liminaries were over.

'We don't see each other any more,' Kate explained unnecessarily.

'I know *that*. I want to know why! One minute Ben's off to buy a ring, then I come home from Mother's to find it's all over. What happened?'

'Perhaps you should ask Ben that.'

Cassie sighed. 'Look, are you going out?'

'No.'

'Can I come round and have a chat? There's some-thing you ought to know. About Ben.'

'What?' said Kate in alarm. 'Is he ill?'

'No, nothing like that. Give me half an hour and I'll be with you.'

By the time Cassie's car drew up outside Waverley Lodge Kate's nerves were in shreds. And even then she had to let Cassie chat for a minute with Mrs Beaumont before getting her upstairs to talk in private.

Kate pulled herself together, made coffee, then sat looking at Cassie, waiting for her to begin. Cassie looked tanned and very attractive, but apart from the all too familiar dark eyes, bore so little resemblance to Ben that it was hard to believe they were brother and sister.

'Right,' Cassie said, sipping her coffee. 'What went wrong?'

Since Kate had said nothing to anyone since the night she parted with Ben, the temptation to confide in someone was suddenly too much to resist. 'He bought me a ring,' she said thickly, and burst into tears.

Cassie dumped her cup down quickly and moved to sit by Kate on the sofa. She took her in her arms and held her close, rocking her as though she were Angus or Emily. 'Go on, love, cry your eyes out. You'll feel better afterwards.'

It was a long time before Kate drew away, eyes swollen and face blotched. 'Sorry, Cassie,' she said at last, drawing in a deep, quivering breath.

'Nothing to be sorry about. At least not to me,' added Cassie wryly. 'Now tell me why the ring was such an insult. Ben said you more or less threw it back in his face and told him to get lost.'

Kate opened her mouth to protest, then scrubbed her eyes with a tissue. 'He made me feel cheap,' she said hoarsely.

'Cheap? My dear girl, Ben's had dozens of girls, but he's never bought a ring for anyone up to now!'

Kate explained, as best she could, what had led up to the night of the break-up, including the lies Dan had fed them about each other.

Cassie stared, open-mouthed. 'You're joking! You actually thought Ben—?' She laughed reluctantly. 'Heavens above, what a poisonous little creep Dan Beaumont is, to be sure. Which brings me to the second reason for my visit.'

'What is it?' said Kate, half hoping there was a message from Ben.

'One of the new software packages—an innovation in the education line—was somehow leaked from Beaumont Electronics to another company. It was Ben's brainchild, he was the only one with access to it, and George Beaumont believes he sold it.' Cassie's lovely mouth tightened dangerously. 'Ben, of all people!'

Kate stared in horror. 'What did he do?'

'Resigned on the spot. Ben's been connected with Beaumont Electronics since he was a student. He took Mr Beaumont's suspicions hard.' Cassie's eyes flashed dangerously. 'When things go wrong for him I get murderous towards the culprit.'

'Is that how you feel towards me?' said Kate forlornly.

Cassie shook her head, smiling warmly. 'No. I admit I didn't feel too kindly towards you at first, which is why I haven't been in contact before. But when I'd cooled down a bit I realised, as Alec firmly pointed out, that you must have had a good reason for turning Ben down.'

'It seemed like a good reason at the time—mainly because I lost my temper,' said Kate bleakly. 'Now I can't imagine why I did such a stupid, hurtful thing. Pride, I suppose. That night I was so happy, Cassie, so much in love with Ben by that time that I was ready to risk moving in with him—'

'Risk?' said Cassie quickly.

Kate nodded. 'I'd been nervous of the idea up to then. Not of the living with Ben part,' she added hastily, 'but of how I would cope when he—when we didn't want to live together any more.'

Cassie's eyes shone with compassion. 'Ah. I see. You felt it wouldn't last.'

'Right. Look at it from my point of view. I'm not exactly Helen of Troy in the looks department, whereas Ben—' She sighed. 'After Ben how could I ever look at any other man? So I took time to weigh up whether a period of my life spent in bliss with him was worth the ultimate pain of how I'd feel once it was all over.' Kate swallowed some coffee convulsively.

'But surely the ring was proof that Ben meant the relationship to be permanent?'

'I didn't see it like that,' said Kate miserably. 'I suppose I was all keyed up to make the move—which, to me, was a far bigger step than just half a mile across town— only to find that Ben thought my consent had a price.'

'Do you still believe that?'

'No. Or if I do I don't care. The only thing that matters is that now I've lost Ben and there's no way of getting him back.' Kate held her head in her hands and began to sob wildly.

Cassie put her arms round her and cuddled her close again. 'If you want my opinion—which you probably don't—all Ben needs is one word, Kate. He's just as miserable as you.'

Kate looked up hopefully, her reddened eyes brightening. Then they dulled again. 'I don't think so, Cassie. I threw a pretty unforgivable parting shot at him that night.'

When Cassie heard the details she had trouble keeping a straight face. 'Oh, dear. Men don't take kindly to doubts of that kind.'

'Especially as I didn't have any. About Ben, I mean,' Kate added, flushing a little. 'But enough about me. Tell me what he's going to do about a job.'

'He's got an interview in London tomorrow, thank goodness. Life's been pretty rough for Ben lately.'

Kate felt utterly sick with remorse. She jumped up suddenly. 'Cassie, will you give me a lift? I'm going to see Ben.'

Cassie got up more slowly, looking doubtful. 'You think that's wise? It might be better to wait until he's got himself sorted out with another job.'

'No!' said Kate vehemently. 'I want to apologise. I *need* to apologise. I just can't wait another night to say I'm sorry. Even if he shuts the door in my face.'

'All right. But if he bites your head off come back to our place for some tea and sympathy. Deal?'

Kate gave a hiccup, and tried to smile. 'Deal!'

Having insisted that Cassie drop her at the bottom of the road, Kate walked towards Ben's flat on leaden feet. What had seemed like the only possible thing to do half an hour earlier now seemed like madness. Ben wouldn't want to look at her, let alone talk to her.

The night was sultry, with threatening dark clouds, in keeping with her mood, and as she approached the tall old house where Ben lived her thin cotton shirt stuck to her back, as much with apprehension as with heat. Kate trudged up the short drive to the front door and rang the bell marked 'Fletcher'. When there was no response her shoulders sagged in despair. After nerving herself to come it was a blow to find that Ben was out. Kate pressed the bell again, but there was no answer, not even barking from Griff.

She brightened. Ben was obviously out walking the dog. She hurried to the carport at the side of the house and found the Range Rover missing. Ben had probably driven Griff to the common, where the dog could run free.

So what now? She could walk home, or go to the Nevilles', or she could wait here. Kate decided to wait. After plucking up enough courage to come it would be a bit lily-livered to turn tail and sneak home again. And a more powerful argument than any was that she just had to see Ben. She couldn't live another night without telling him she was sorry, even if he threw her out afterwards and told her never to darken his door again. After a long day on her feet in the shop, Kate longed to sit down, and as Ben's garden lacked a seat she flopped down on the grass under the big beech tree near the gate and settled herself to wait.

During her fortnight at home in Guildford it had been hot and sunny almost every day. To pass the time Kate had helped with the gardening, and sunbathed as much as possible, and as a result the legs stretched below her brief denim skirt were a very satisfactory shade of brown. Her old white tennis shirt and grubby pink sneakers were less appealing. But once the decision was made she'd only taken time to braid her damp hair before rushing Cassie out of the house to drive her here. Which made it all the more of an anticlimax to find Ben missing.

Minutes dragged by, then suddenly the leaves began to rustle ominously in the sheltering beech tree and rain began to pelt down. Kate jumped to her feet and stood shivering, suddenly cold as the temperature dropped. Soaked through very quickly, she was on the point of going home after all, when a crack of thunder changed her mind, sending her running to the covered carport for shelter. The storm gathered force; rain hammered on the corrugated glass roof and flashes of lightning illu-

minated the entire garden, by which time Kate was bitterly regretting her impulse.

After what felt like hours she decided to brave the
elements and walk home. The storm was passing, and
she could hardly get much colder and wetter than she
was already. Then headlights sent her shrinking back for
cover as the Range Rover turned into the drive. Ben had
come home at last. And now he was here she wanted
nothing more than to run for home before he discovered
her.

Kate flattened herself against the side wall as the passenger door of the Range Rover came to a stop in front
of her nose. She stood motionless, afraid to breathe.
Ben got out of the car without noticing her, but Griff
leapt out after him, and with a sharp bark he raced round
the car and found Kate. For a moment the dog stood
still, legs stiff, growling menacingly. Then he sniffed and
bounded towards her, frisking like a puppy.

'Griff! Heel!' ordered Ben sternly, and obediently the
dog settled himself at Kate's wet feet. Ben strode round
the car to investigate, his tall shape menacing in the semi-
darkness. 'Who—?' He stopped dead. '*Kate?* What the
devil are you playing at? I've been searching everywhere
for you!'

Since this was the last thing she'd expected Kate was
temporarily struck dumb.

'Where the hell have you been?' he demanded irritably.

'Guildford,' she managed hoarsely.

He shook his head impatiently. 'I meant tonight! I
called in at Cassie's on my way back from the common
with Griff and she said you'd come to see me. You
weren't here when I got back so I went to your place,
and Mrs Beaumont said you'd gone off with my sister

and were still out. I've been driving round in circles looking for you.'

'Why?' said Kate, surprised.

'Because Cassie asked me to,' he said cruelly. 'Why else? Anyway, where the hell were you?'

'Here. I was tired when I got here so I decided to sit under the tree until you turned up. Then the storm broke and I got wet so I sheltered under the carport.' Her voice wavered a little. 'If you could just call a cab for me I'll get off home. It must be late.'

'Don't be stupid! If you're wet you'd better dry off, have a hot drink. Besides,' he added coldly, 'I want to know what brought you here tonight. You must have had some reason for coming.'

If she had, thought Kate resentfully as she squelched after him into the house, it was beginning to feel like a very silly one by this time. She'd come to say she was sorry, her heart wrung by the story Cassie had told her. In her mind she'd pictured Ben at a low ebb, after his resignation from Beaumont Electronics. But nothing was further from the truth, she realised as she walked barefoot into Ben's brightly lit kitchen.

He was dressed in ordinary grey jogging pants and a white sweatshirt, but, as always, just to look at him made her heart turn somersaults. His damp, untidy hair, and the smudges of fatigue under his eyes, only added to the general charisma. While she, Kate thought glumly, looked like a drowned rat. She held out the grubby wet sneakers by their laces.

'Could I put these somewhere to drip? Your carport had a sort of river running through it during the storm.'

Ben took them without comment, crumpled some kitchen paper and thrust it in the toes of the shoes, then put them on the draining-board. He filled the kettle, plugged it in, then turned to look at her, his mouth tightening as he took in her bedraggled state.

'Go and have a hot shower,' he ordered. 'You're shivering. I'll find you something to wear.'

None of this fitted Kate's original plan. But something in Ben's manner quashed all protest. In the bathroom she wrapped a towel round her wet head and stood under water as hot as she could bear, then secured a bathsheet under her arms, freed her hair from its braid and dried it a little with another towel, wondering what to do next. At Ben's knock she opened the door a crack and a long hand slid round it, holding a sweatshirt and a pair of striped boxer shorts.

'Best I can do,' he said gruffly, and went off again.

Kate, indifferent to anything as trivial as vanity by this time, pulled on the shorts, grateful that Ben was narrow-hipped. She added the thick, all-enveloping white sweatshirt, which reached almost to her knees, then borrowed Ben's hairbrush to tame her hair into something like order. Afterwards she washed the hairbrush punctiliously, gathered up her wet clothes and went back to the kitchen, where of the two waiting for her only Griff appeared pleased.

If she had hopes that her bizarre appearance might soften Ben's attitude towards her, they were soon dashed. He gave an order to the dog, then led the way to the sitting room, where the curtains were drawn and the lamps lit to shut out the weather outside. The room, thought Kate, looked like a stage set, waiting for the actors to make their entrance. A tea-tray waited on the low table in front of the sofa.

'I thought you'd prefer tea at this time of night,' said Ben.

'Thank you. Are you having something?'

He indicated the glass of whisky on the table beside him. 'So,' he said, without any preliminaries, 'why are you here, Kate?'

Good question, she thought, pouring the tea. It had seemed the only possible thing to do earlier. But that was with a dejected, embattled Ben in her mind's eye. Ben in the flesh was cold and collected and, if appearances were anything to go by, in no need of sympathy at all.

'I came to apologise,' she said after a while, forcing herself to meet his eyes squarely. 'Last time we saw each other I behaved abominably. I'm sorry.'

She saw a tiny pulse throbbing beside Ben's mouth and felt better. Underneath the hostile mask he was no more calm and collected than she was.

'Does the apology apply to everything that happened that night?' he asked carefully.

Kate thought about it. 'Yes. We somehow got our lines of communication snarled up a bit. Afterwards I realised that any other female would have been turning cartwheels for joy in that particular situation.'

'But you had to be different,' he said sardonically. 'Which, of course, is why I bought the ring. Because you were different.'

'The timing was wrong,' she muttered, flushing.

'Have you any idea,' he asked conversationally, 'what it was like to get my ring thrown back in my face? I admit I bought it on impulse. I was in London with time to kill before catching the train back. I needed a new strap for my watch, and there in the jeweller's was the ring. It suddenly seemed so simple. It would show you, I thought with crass male stupidity, exactly what you meant to me.'

Kate was feeling worse by the minute. 'I just wish you'd given it to me later.'

'How much later?'

'After we'd actually begun to live together,' she said miserably.

'Ah, but at that particular moment in time I had no idea that you were about to unbend and deign to grace my bed and board,' he said harshly.

Kate finished her tea and stood up, looking up to meet his eyes when he promptly rose to his feet too. 'Time I went. I came to apologise, so once again I'm sorry, not only about the ring but also about my cheap parting shot. I was angry and I wanted to hurt.'

'You succeeded.'

'In hurting myself too, if that's of any interest to you,' she said quietly. 'May I ring for a cab? I'm afraid I'll have to borrow these things to go home. I'll launder them and send them back.'

'I'll drive you home,' Ben said quickly. 'I haven't touched the whisky.'

It seemed ungracious to refuse. Kate nodded politely. 'Thank you. Whenever you're ready, then.'

'Sit down and drink some more tea.' As he sat down again his eyes softened a little. 'You look about twelve in that get-up with your hair hanging down—' He stopped abruptly, reached for the whisky, changed his mind and put it down again, and Kate hurriedly poured herself more tea.

'Actually,' she said, clearing her throat, 'there was something else I wanted to say. Cassie told me what happened at Beaumont's.'

His eyes iced over again. 'Ah! So that's why you came—to commiserate.'

'Partly, yes. It's all a lot of nonsense and anyone who knows you will think the same,' she said flatly.

'Up to now no one does know, apart from George Beaumont. Everyone else in the firm thinks I want to make a career move.' He shrugged grimly. 'Maybe it's a good thing. I've lived most of my life here in Pennington. It's probably time I dug myself out of a rut. Tomorrow I hope to convince a London firm of both my technical brilliance and my impeachable integrity. George Beaumont's prepared to give me a glowing reference for old times' sake—provided I push off and set up my stall somewhere else.'

'It's not fair!' said Kate with sudden passion.

'Life isn't fair. Besides, pastures new seem like a good idea under the circumstances,' said Ben, giving her a look which left her in no doubt as to why.

Kate finished her tea in silence, feeling suddenly horribly weary. The bright determination which had led her here had long since vanished, leaving her with a heavy, flat feeling of disappointment. But what had she expected? It had been naïve of her to hope that Ben would take one look at his scruffy, bedraggled visitor and sweep her into his arms, declaring that all was forgiven. She sighed. What a fool!

'That was a heartfelt sigh,' he commented.

Kate smiled brightly. 'It's late. I must go. Sorry to drag you out again—'

'Not at all,' he said politely, as though they were strangers. 'Thank you for taking the trouble to come.'

'I hadn't bargained on it being quite as *much* trouble,' she said less meekly. 'It was a rather nice evening when I started out. I should have paid more attention to the weather forecast.'

'But it's supposed to be a fine day tomorrow, and the outlook for the rest of the week is quite good—sunny spells with occasional showers,' he said, tongue-in-cheek. 'Right, that's finished the weather. Now what shall we talk about?'

'I've run out of polite conversation,' she said with sudden heat. 'I'd like to go home, please.'

Ben rose to his feet, smiling sardonically as he held out his hand to help her up. 'That's more like it. I thought the penitent mood wouldn't last long.'

She glared up at him, ignoring the hand as she jumped up. 'It wasn't easy to come here to apologise, you know!'

'I do know, and I appreciate it. But tell the truth, Kate—would you have come if Cassie hadn't told you I had to resign from Beaumont's?'

She hesitated, then shook her head. 'No, Ben. I was sure you'd shut the door in my face.'

He took her hand. 'I could never do that, Kate. Actually I was so shattered by the whole damn business at Beaumont's, I called to see you one evening last week, needing salve for my wounds. I met Gail coming out of Hardacres and she told me you were away on holiday until today.'

'She didn't tell me!'

Ben's mouth twisted. 'She's never forgiven me, has she?'

'Or me either. She's young. Forgiveness is hard at her age, especially with a man like you.'

'Like me?' he said quickly, and Kate smiled a little.

'I'm afraid Gail nourishes a hopeless passion for you—though who am I to say it's hopeless?'

'You know it is, beyond all doubt,' he said wearily, and took her in his arms. He kissed her—a long, oddly passionless kiss—then put her away from him so suddenly that she staggered a little.

'I didn't mean to do that.'

'Because I'm still unforgiven?' she said shakily.

'No. Because I need to sort my life out professionally before I allow myself the luxury of even thinking about you, Kate.'

'I suppose what happened with me seems pretty silly and unimportant compared with the other problem,' she said, mortified.

Ben shook his hair back from his face. 'Hell, no. It's done a lot for my morale to have you come here tonight. Tomorrow I've got only the second job interview I've ever needed in my life to date.'

'You're bound to be successful,' she assured him.

'I have to be.'

'Why?'

His smile lacked the casual *savoir-faire* of before. Ben Fletcher had hardened during the weeks of their separation. The smile he gave her now was that of a man determined to survive whatever fate threw at him.

'I'll tell you why when I've succeeded. Come and say goodnight to Griff.' Ben laughed suddenly. 'You look like jail-bait in that get-up—which is why I prefer to see you safely home myself.'

'I'm twenty-seven and a very sober citizen,' she said mock-wrathfully, secretly so relieved to have Ben in thawing mood that she could have jumped for joy. 'I'll just try and push my feet into my sneakers.'

Ben watched her struggle, holding Griff away from his deep interest in the exercise. 'I could have told you it was no use,' he informed her, and gave her a large polythene bag. 'Put your gear in there and I'll carry you to the car.'

This was a process which had rendered them both breathless by the time Kate was installed in the Range Rover. She sat, fists clenched, trying to hide the turbulence inside her as Ben got in the car. He drove her home in silence, just as he'd done on that other, doomed evening, but this time the silence was different. When they arrived at Waverley Lodge it was in darkness, for which Kate was profoundly thankful. She turned to Ben in sudden compunction. 'Ben! I forgot to ring Cassie. She must be worried.'

'I rang her when you were in the shower,' he assured her.

'I don't know what's the matter with me,' she said bitterly. 'My brain isn't functioning properly.'

'Maybe the same thing that's affecting me,' said Ben huskily, and took her in his arms. 'I want you like hell, Kate. Have you any idea what the sight of you did to me tonight? That sodden shirt was sticking to you like a second skin. I had to fight myself tooth and nail not to throw you on the kitchen floor there and then!' He kissed her fiercely, and this time the barriers came down, all the pent-up feelings of the past few weeks bursting through as they strained closer to each other. Kate trembled wildly as his hands slid beneath the sweatshirt, her own locking behind his neck as she arched her back in response to his caresses.

'I promised myself I wouldn't do this,' he breathed against her throat at last. 'Not now, not yet.'

'When, then?' she said militantly. 'Don't tell me you've got some quixotic idea about clearing your name, like something from a Victorian novel. Life's too short, Ben. I know you didn't do it; so does your family. Who else matters?' She thrust her hands in his hair and brought his mouth to hers, and they held each other in fierce, glad reunion until a church clock striking one brought them back to earth.

Ben carried Kate up to her door, unlocked it and set her down on the hall carpet. 'I'll be away for three days,' he said softly. 'I've got a few contacts to look up.'

'What's happening to Griff?'

'He's off to the Neville household. I'll ring you when I get back.'

She nodded. 'See that you do or I'll camp out on your doorstep again.'

He kissed her hard. 'I couldn't believe my luck when I found a sodden, shivering little bundle hiding in my carport.'

'You were horribly distant!'

'Is that surprising after our last encounter?' he said grimly, then kissed her again at some length. 'As I've said before, Kate Harker, I'm only human.'

'Me too,' she said, hugging him close. 'And good luck. Not that you need it.' She then muttered something unintelligible into his chest, and Ben held her away from him.

'What did you say?'

'I'll tell you when you come back.'

CHAPTER TWELVE

IT WAS a different, secretly jubilant Kate who returned to Hardacres next day. After setting up the points of sale and installing the day's cash float she beckoned to Gail and took her aside.

'I appreciate your problem in this particular instance, Gail, but in future please tell me when anyone asks for me or leaves a message for me, no matter who it is. Do I make myself clear?'

Gail flushed and nodded guiltily, but Kate smiled briskly to show that no harm was done, and for the rest of the day Gail worked hard, over and above the call of duty, eager to make reparation. Or afraid for her job, thought Kate the realist.

Kate asked Clare to postpone their usual visit to the cinema that night.

'Of course,' said Clare, eyeing Kate curiously. 'Why? Got a better offer?'

Kate smiled demurely. 'I'm working on it.'

She went out alone in her lunch-hour, making for the Pergola, a rather smart wine-bar popular with some of the younger business set for lunch. She chose a small table in the window, ordered mineral water and a salad, opened the book she'd brought with her and settled down to wait. As she'd hoped, Dan Beaumont came in with a group of cronies while she was eating her lunch. Kate kept her eyes glued to her book, and right on cue Dan noticed her and promptly came over.

'All alone?' he asked, grinning down at her.

'My friend stood me up,' she fibbed, making a face. 'Hello, Dan.'

'Long time no see,' said Dan, as breezily as though the hassle of their last encounter had never happened. 'What's happened to Big Ben? I thought you two lived in each other's pockets these days.'

Kate, marvelling at her acting skills, gave him a saucy little smile. 'You're behind the times. Haven't seen him for ages.' Which until the night before had been true enough.

Dan was bad at hiding his feelings. At this piece of news his face lit up, and he took the seat opposite, clicking his fingers for one of the young waiters to bring his lunch across. Without asking her, as usual, Kate noted with hostility.

'Well, well, this *is* a surprise,' he said, tucking into a beef sandwich. 'You don't usually come here.'

'It's a bit expensive for me,' she said sadly. 'My friend was treating me today, otherwise I'd have stayed in the staffroom as usual. With Clare,' she added.

Dan's eyes flickered. 'Who's Clare?'

'My colleague at work—the tall, auburn-haired one. Only she won't be working much longer. She's expecting a baby.'

'Good for her,' said Dan, and hurriedly changed the subject to his grandmother, transparent in his ploy to remind Kate that they had a common link. They chatted about Mrs Beaumont, about the heatwave, then Kate stood up.

'Time to go, I'm afraid.'

Dan jumped to his feet, looking, for Dan, oddly uncertain. 'Look, Kate, I'm sorry about what happened.

I was a damn fool. But you're a very attractive lady—
you can't blame a chap for trying.'

She smiled at him forgivingly. 'Let's forget it, shall
we?'

He brightened. 'You're a great girl, Kate. Have dinner
with me tonight!' He smiled cajolingly. 'Go on. Say yes!'

Kate pretended to think it over, then looked at him
from under her lashes. 'I might. On one condition. No
more rough stuff.'

Dan shook his head vigorously. 'I'll be good as gold.
Scout's honour.'

'Don't tell me you were a Boy Scout, Dan Beaumont,'
she scoffed, and he laughed uproariously.

'Me? No way! But I meant what I said. I won't step
out of line, I promise.'

Kate got ready for her evening with great care, a light
in her eye which, if he'd known her better, would have
warned Dan Beaumont to tread warily. Her dress was
an old favourite, made of thin lawn the colour of ter-
racotta, with a low, dipping neckline to show off her
tan. It fastened with a row of small gilt buttons, the last
few of which Kate left undone from just above the knee.
She put on flat gold sandals, to flatter Dan's lack of
inches, and released her hair in loose ripples from the
tight braid she'd kept it in all day.

She then went to work on her tanned face, accen-
tuating her eyes with smudges of grey shadow, two coats
of mascara on her lashes, and did some close work with
a lip-liner and brush to make her mouth look like a ripe
peach. Finally Kate fastened gold hoops in her ears, and
gave her reflection a satisfied little smile. It was Carmen
all over again on a less spectacular scale.

Dan Beaumont was lavish with his compliments when he came to collect her. He was dressed to kill himself, in a sky-blue jacket over white T-shirt and jeans, and talked his head off as he drove her out into the Gloucestershire countryside. At any other time his febrile laughter and flow of one-liners would have got on Kate's nerves, but tonight she egged him on, laughing at his jokes, looking deeply impressed when he bragged about his latest plans for his father's company.

He was obviously well-known at the inn he'd chosen. They were given the best table in the dining room and this time Dan consulted her about her drinks and her choice of meal, pulling out all the stops to please her. Kate let him fuss over her, and chose the salmon, as he urged her to, and drank a little of the expensive wine. Fortunately, because Dan seemed to need several trips to the men's room, Kate was able to dispose of the major part of her wine into a very convenient flowering plant in the window embrasure. Dan himself drank very little, assuring her that he took no chances with the drink-driving laws, but each time he returned to the table he was a little more animated, his eyes brighter.

As they drove back through the starlit night Dan licked his lips, eyeing her from time to time, as though he had something to ask. At last he blurted it out.

'Come back to my place. Please, Kate.'

She hid her triumph behind demure hesitation. 'Oh, I don't know about that, Dan. I've got work to-morrow—'

'So have I,' he broke in eagerly. 'Just half an hour. I'll take you home afterwards, I promise.'

Dan's flat was just what Kate had expected: white carpets, glass tables, furniture upholstered in black

Italian leather. He waved her to a couch, then excused himself for a while.

Wanting badly to turn tail and run, Kate had to make herself sit down, reminding herself forcibly that she was here for Ben's sake. It was a role she had to play. Even so it was hard to summon up an encouraging smile when Dan came back.

'Have a drink!' he urged.

Kate let him give her a brandy, then stiffened in utter horror as Dan shook some powder onto a low table, scraped it in lines and rolled up a twenty-pound note. Feeling sick, she managed to hide her revulsion by the time he turned round to her with a sly grin. 'Fancy some, Kate? It's the best, I promise.'

'Not for me, thanks—but you go ahead.' She gave him a brilliant smile to mask her distaste and settled lower on the couch, crossing her legs so that the dress fell away. Dan sniffed up a line of cocaine and breathed in deeply, eyes closed for a minute before they opened again, their febrile glitter brighter than ever.

'I always knew we'd be good together if you'd give me a chance.' He sat down beside her, put an arm round her and leaned back.

Kate slid a hand into the pocket let into the side seam of her dress, forcing herself to cuddle closer. She felt Dan relax as he started talking again, his confidences tumbling out in familiar, braggart style: how clever he'd been at college, how brilliant he was at his job, and how much the company would improve now Ben Fletcher was leaving.

'Is he really?' said Kate with artistic surprise, wanting to kill Dan Beaumont. 'I thought he was your father's right-hand man.'

'The gospel according to St Benedict, I suppose!' he sneered, and gave an evil little chuckle. 'Actually he was—until I joined the firm. Now it's different.'

'Why's he leaving?' she asked casually.

'Got the push!' Dan chortled loudly, then took his arm away, leaned over and inhaled another line of powder from the table. He turned glazed eyes on Kate, laughing crazily at the look of eager curiosity on her face.

'Do tell,' she urged. 'I thought he was Mr Perfect. Did your father interrupt something with Ben and one of his—er—friends?'

Dan licked his lips, his eyes glistening. 'Worse than that, my poppet. Ben sold his pet project to a rival software company.'

'No!' Please forgive me, Ben, prayed Kate as she put her head on Dan's shoulder, pretending to shake with laughter. 'You're kidding me!'

Dan put his arms round her, rocking her against him in an ecstasy of mirth. 'I'm not! I hated Ben Fletcher from the first day I saw him,' he said viciously. 'Too tall, too good-looking and too damn good at his job. But I soon put a stop to that—' He paused, and Kate steeled herself to melt against him.

'How ever did you do that?' she said, gazing up at him in limpid admiration.

'Secret,' he said, tapping his nose. He winked. 'My secret.'

Kate had known from the first that Dan had to be the culprit, but she felt a surge of triumph to have it confirmed. She smiled slowly, running the tip of her tongue over her lips. 'Who's a clever boy, then?' she crooned, and he seized her in his arms, grinding his mouth against hers. She forced herself to respond, to pretend she was eager for his hot, damp hands and wet, seeking mouth. Soon he was panting, urging her to come to bed, but Kate held him off, smiling sultrily into his dilated eyes.

'Not yet, Danny boy.'

'What are you holding out for?' he panted, tugging at her dress.

She pulled away, tapping his cheek playfully. 'It's a secret. And you've got to guess it before...' She leaned forward, mouth parted, running her fingers up and down his thigh.

'I can't!' he gasped, reaching for her.

Kate arched away, so that the upper curves of her breasts showed above the neckline of her dress. 'All right, then. You tell me your secret and I'll tell you mine.'

'Easy!' He gave a cracked laugh of triumph. 'I was going to anyway. I've got to tell someone or I'll burst. It was brilliant!' He seized her by the waist, his eyes glittering triumphantly into hers. 'I was sick of Ben Fletcher and his marvellous new software brainchild. So I copied it and gave it to an old mate from college. He paid me in cash—lots of it—then passed it on to his bosses, got a bonus for being such a clever boy, and everyone was happy.'

'Gosh!' said Kate in exaggerated admiration. 'That was clever. How did your father find out?'

'He read about the other firm's new program in the paper. And thought exactly what I wanted him to think— that Ben was the only one who could have done it. No one else had access to the program.'

'So how did you manage it?'

He gave a wild bray of laughter. 'I stole back into work, night after night—the security people thought nothing of the owner's son doing a bit of overtime. Beautiful, wasn't it? I hacked into his computer until at last I cracked it. Ben Fletcher's not the only brain at Beaumont's.' His eyes narrowed. 'So come on—stop messing about, Kate. What's your secret?'

Kate got to her feet, the alluring compliance falling away from her like a cloak. 'It's the same as yours,' she said coldly, and picked up her bag.

Dan's jaw dropped, then his colour flared and he dived for her, but Kate sidestepped as neatly as a rugby fly-half and he sprawled full length on the carpet. He scrambled up, snarling, but she whipped a small recording machine from her pocket and stopped him dead in his tracks.

'Every word is on tape in here— Oh, no, you don't,' she warned, dancing out of reach as he lunged for it. 'Now listen, Dan Beaumont, and listen well. You're going to tell your father exactly what you did. If not I'll give this to the Press and tell them you were snorting coke and threatened to assault me.'

'You bitch!' howled Dan in outrage.

'Just call me Nemesis, Dan,' she said sweetly, and nodded towards the phone. 'Pick that up and ring him now. Tell him it was you, not Ben. If not I'll deliver this to the Press. Choose. Brownie points for your penitent confession to Daddy, or risk his reaction to the tabloid version.' Kate dodged away as he again tried to snatch the recorder from her. 'No chance, Dan.' She put it in her handbag and tugged the zip shut.

Suddenly Dan, his mental and physical reactions distorted by the drug, crumpled like a pricked balloon. He slumped into a chair, crying like a baby. 'Why?' he sobbed. 'Why are you doing this?'

'Because I want Ben Fletcher's name cleared,' she said very deliberately, hoping Dan couldn't tell she was shaking like a leaf inside. 'His career could have been ruined. Yours won't be because you're Daddy's little boy. So do it, Dan. Pick up that phone. Keep on with the tears, though. Nice touch. They might convince your father you regret what you did.'

'Give me that blasted tape first!'

'No way. I keep that as my insurance policy. I'll put it in a very safe place, I promise. So get on with it!' Kate picked up the phone and punched in the number she'd already memorised, waited until George Beaumont answered, then handed the instrument to Dan.

Kate stood over Dan Beaumont while he made his hoarse, reluctant confession to his father. When he put the phone down with a shaking hand at last, Dan's face was ghastly, his red-rimmed eyes filled with hatred as he glared at Kate.

'Are you happy now?' he spat.

'No, Dan. I'm deeply sorry for your father. You've been spoiled rotten. He should have taken a strap to you years ago.'

He swallowed sickly. 'I'd prefer that to what he just said to me. He wants to see me first thing in the morning, God help me.' Suddenly his swollen, bloodshot eyes narrowed. 'How do I know you won't use the tape to blackmail me in the future?'

'Don't judge everyone by your own standards, Dan. Believe me, I won't. Look on this as a learning exercise,' said Kate. Her cold eyes locked with his. 'Ben's the only one I'll tell about my visit here tonight. Let's hope he doesn't forget himself and try a little corporal punishment by way of retribution. Have you forgotten all those sickening lies you told about Ben—*and* me? Did you really think you could get away with it all? Take your medicine like a man, Daniel Beaumont. Nothing's for nothing in this life.'

'What I don't understand,' he said venomously, 'is what *you* get out of this—why the hell you went to all this trouble.'

Kate shook her head pityingly. 'It's very simple, Dan. I did it for love.'

Ben had rung her from London to say that he'd pick her up from Hardacres on the evening of his return, and it was just gone six when the familiar Range Rover arrived outside the shop. Gail, who had taken Kate's lecture to heart, came running to fetch her from the upper floor and Mrs Harrison waved Kate off with a benevolent smile.

'Off you go, Kate. I'll lock up tonight.'

Kate rushed into the staffroom for her bag, then bade everyone a joyous goodnight and hurried through the last-minute crowd of customers to the tall figure waiting at the door.

Ben's face lit with the usual heart-stopping smile as he bent to kiss her, oblivious of their audience. He rushed her into the car, then drove home to his flat, refusing to say a word about his trip. He had such a look of suppressed excitement about him that Kate felt sparks would fly if she so much as touched him.

Once inside the flat he pulled her into his arms and kissed her at length, and they were both gasping by the time he set her free.

'You obviously got the job,' she said breathlessly.

Ben laughed. 'There was a message on my Ansaphone when I got in. They want me as soon as I can make it. Where shall we go to celebrate?'

'Somewhere near, where we can walk back; then you can have a drink to celebrate too,' said Kate, hugging him.

Ben held her away from him. 'I'd still have to drive you home.'

'Not necessarily.'

His eyes gleamed. 'Why, Miss Harker, are you proposing we spend the night together?' When she nodded he pulled her close to kiss her again.

'If you don't stop we won't get out at all,' she said breathlessly.

'True.' His lips twitched. 'At least we don't have a chaperon tonight. Griff's still with Cassie. So let's eat ham and eggs at the Barley Mow, then come back and go to bed. We've got time to make up.'

The programme met with such shameless enthusiasm from Kate that it was some time before they actually started out to Ben's local. As they strolled, hand in hand, Kate listened to his account of the interview, smiling up at him so raptly that Ben told her at one stage to stop it—she was wrecking his concentration.

'This is a quiet part of town,' he said, grinning. 'I'll shock the residents if I make love to you on the pavement.'

The pub was unpretentious, but the simple food was perfectly cooked, and Kate drank lager shandy and felt so happy to be with Ben that nothing mattered other than their being together at last. They sat close together on one of the settles while Ben discussed the new job and impressed her by the rise in salary it would mean for him.

'But,' he said triumphantly, when they were walking back to the flat, 'I've kept the best news of all until we were alone again.'

Kate looked up at him expectantly. 'Don't keep me in suspense, Ben Fletcher!'

Ben told her how another message had been waiting for him on his return. 'I got back about two, to find George Beaumont wanted an urgent word with me. I rang him and he asked to see me. I offered to drive in straight away, but to my surprise he asked me to his house. He said it was too important to talk about in his office. When I got there I was shocked. He looked terrible—years older, like a man who'd just suffered a bereavement. He told me he'd accused me unjustly of a crime his son confessed to a couple of days ago.'

'So it was Dan,' said Kate, glad that they were walking side by side so he couldn't see her face.

'You don't sound surprised.'

'I'm not. Who else could it have been?'

'But I was always so careful with security. And with something revolutionary like this particular program I'd taken extra care. But the clever little so-and-so managed to hack into it just the same, and passed it on to a pal of his, who, needless to say, works for the people now manufacturing my brainchild. I gather Dan got a nice little pay-off.'

'The horrible little toad!' said Kate passionately, needing no acting to convey her loathing for Dan Beaumont. 'What are you going to do?'

'About Dan, nothing. No one at the firm knows that I resigned, so if I like I can just go back, pretend I took a break, and carry on the same as before.'

'Is that what you want to do?' asked Kate, once they were back in the flat.

Ben sat down with her on his lap, rubbing his cheek over her hair. 'No, it's not. I could make life very difficult for young Dan, of course, and take pleasure in it. But I won't because he owned up in the end, though his father was a bit cagey about why he confessed. Not like Dan at all. Anyway, I owe George Beaumont a lot; he's been good to me. In fact, in some ways, that's the worst part of it all. He begged me not to reveal the truth about his son, confided in me to a degree that makes it impossible for me to go back anyway. We could never be comfortable together again. Apparently, just between you and me, Dan has a drug problem.'

'That doesn't surprise me,' said Kate, with truth. 'His behaviour rather bears that out, doesn't it? I'm sorry for Mr Beaumont, but it seems a shame that Dan gets off scot-free.'

'He doesn't. He's off to some detox centre, apparently.'

'You could have been awkward,' she pointed out.

'I know. But I'd be hurting Dan's family more than him, so I thought, To hell with it. I've got a new job, completely on my own merits, with nothing more than a good reference from Beaumont's to help me on my way. I couldn't make my old boss suffer for the sins of his son. I told him the secret would be safe with me.'

And mine will be safe with me, thought Kate. Contrary to what she'd said to Dan, she would never tell Ben about her part in clearing his name, because that would entail confessing that she'd practically seduced Dan into telling her he was the culprit. And Ben, as he'd told her several times, was only human, and a male human at that. He'd be livid. Might not forgive her, even. And no way was she risking that.

'I brought you a present from London,' said Ben, breaking into her reverie.

Kate smiled up at him in pleasure. 'Goody. I love presents.'

'You didn't like the last one!'

'I did. I explained all that.' She reached up and kissed him. 'I'm sorry I was such a pig.'

'I'm glad you're suitably repentant,' he said mockingly, and took a small leather box from his pocket, opened it, and took her left hand, sliding a ring onto her third finger.

Kate gazed at the diamond and sapphire ring through a fog of tears.

'If you throw this one back at me I give up,' said Ben, not quite jokingly.

Kate threw her arms round him instead, muttering incoherently into his neck, and Ben turned her face up to his and kissed her very thoroughly. He raised his head at last, and looked down at her rather sternly.

'It's a ring, Kate. Nothing more sinister than that. I'm not binding you to anything. Yet. I just want you in my life on a permanent basis.'

'I'm happy with that,' she assured him unsteadily, and lifted her hand to gaze at the ring. 'What happened to the other one?'

'I exchanged it.' He smiled crookedly. 'I couldn't stand the sight of it once you gave it back. My ego couldn't cope.'

Kate got to her feet and held out her hand. 'It must have been a blow to someone who looks like you—not that anyone does,' she added. 'You're unique.'

He leapt up and caught her in his arms, kissing her all the way upstairs to his bedroom. He laid her down on the bed, and stretched out beside her. 'Kate, let's get something straight. My looks are an accident of nature. In some ways they've been a handicap. It's taken me until now to find the one woman in the world I want to share my life with. I'll never do anything to jeopardise that, darling.'

Kate moved into his embrace, kissing him with such uninhibited fervour that they were soon caught up in the passion they'd been holding at bay all evening. This time, there was no frenzy of shocked discovery; they took unhurried, mutual pleasure in discovering what pleased the other most, sharing both laughter and rapture on their way to fulfilment as they celebrated the first night of the rest of their lives.

Ben held her close in the darkness afterwards, raising the hand with the ring to his lips. 'There's something I should have said earlier, when I put this on your finger. I love you, Katherine Harker. Do you love me?'

Kate lay very still, her heart pounding in her chest.

'Did you hear me?' he demanded.

'Yes.' She buried her face in his neck. 'Oh, Ben, of course I do. That's what I said just before you left the other night.'

'I hoped it was. How much?' he whispered.

'More than you'll ever know,' she assured him passionately.

And he never would if she could help it, thought Kate. There was one secret she would never share with Ben.

'If you'd said you loved me when you gave me the first ring,' she informed him, 'I wouldn't have given it back.'

Ben shook her slightly. 'The ring was supposed to say that for me.' He paused. 'I want you to apply for a transfer and come to London with me.'

'Right.'

'And one day, I warn you, I'm going to give you a plain gold ring to go with that one.'

'Good idea.'

'You're very malleable tonight.' He chuckled, but his arms tightened at her prompt response.

'It probably won't last!' she warned him, laughing.

'Then I'll make the most of it while I can. Take the day off tomorrow!'

'Yes,' she said submissively, then spoilt it by giggling. 'I already have.'

'You hussy. Did you know I wanted to stay in bed with you all day?'

'No. But I hoped. Though we ought to visit the Neville household at some stage.'

Ben settled her against him more comfortably. 'Cassie is sure to be pleased. She told me I was a fool not to make up before.'

'So why didn't you?'

'I was on the point of it when you came back to me, darling.'

'Were you really?' Kate gave an ecstatic little wriggle. 'I want to believe you, so I will.'

'Very magnanimous!'

'Not that it matters who made up, as long as one of us did.' Kate smoothed his hair back with a loving hand. 'They say love is never having to say sorry, but I think it's a good idea now and again.'

Ben caught the hand and kissed it. 'So do I. A good relationship is a give and take affair on both sides, with no murky secrets lurking in the background. We had to fight our way past a couple of those to get to where we are now. So from now on no more, agreed?'

From now on, thought Kate. This she could swear to. She looked him straight in the eye and laid a hand on her heart. 'Agreed, Benedict Fletcher. From this day forward no more secrets. Ever.'

MILLS & BOON®

Next Month's Romances

♡

Each month you can choose from a wide variety of romance with Mills & Boon. Below are the new titles to look out for next month in our two new series Presents and Enchanted.

Presents™

THEIR WEDDING DAY	Emma Darcy
THE FINAL PROPOSAL	Robyn Donald
HIS BABY!	Sharon Kendrick
MARRIED FOR REAL	Lindsay Armstrong
MISTLETOE MAN	Kathleen O'Brien
BAD INFLUENCE	Susanne McCarthy
TORN BY DESIRE	Natalie Fox
POWERFUL PERSUASION	Margaret Mayo

Enchanted™

THE VICAR'S DAUGHTER	Betty Neels
BECAUSE OF THE BABY	Debbie Macomber
UNEXPECTED ENGAGEMENT	Jessica Steele
BORROWED WIFE	Patricia Wilson
ANGEL BRIDE	Barbara McMahon
A WIFE FOR CHRISTMAS	Pamela Bauer & Judy Kaye
ALL SHE WANTS FOR CHRISTMAS	Liz Fielding
TROUBLE IN PARADISE	Grace Green

MAL

How to enter...

There are two five letter words provided in the grid overleaf. The first one being STOCK the other PLATE. All you have to do is write down the words that are missing by changing just one letter at a time to form a new word and eventually change the word STOCK into PLATE. You only have eight chances but we have supplied you with clues as to what each one is. Good Luck!

When you have completed the grid don't forget to fill in your name and address in the space provided below and pop this page into an envelope (you don't even need a stamp) and post it today. Hurry—competition ends 31st May 1997.

Mills & Boon® Singie Letter Switch
FREEPOST
Croydon
Surrey
CR9 3WZ

Are you a Reader Service Subscriber?   Yes ❑   No ❑

Ms/Mrs/Miss/Mr _____

Address _____

_____

_____ Postcode _____

One application per household.

You may be mailed with other offers from other reputable companies as a result of this application. If you would prefer not to receive such offers, please tick box.   ❑

C6K